DOCTOR MATE

JAMESON PACK

K.A. BAUER

JUST A HEADS UP:

The events of this book take place simultaneously with the events of the Alpha's Little Psycho series and continue on after the end of the events of those books. If you have not read the series, you should still be able to enjoy this series on its own, but please be aware that there may be some events and scenes that are only explained fully in the other series. There will definitely be crossovers from Ethan and Ric and Jack throughout the Jameson Pack series.

Thank you and I hope you enjoy how Fate works in the Jameson Pack.

1

CONNOR

Twenty One Years Ago

There's a lot of noise downstairs. I'm supposed to be sleeping, but I'm curious. Daddy was talking to a vampire the other day and then I woke up the next morning to a baby brother.

I'm a big brother now!

Mommy and Daddy are being mean to each other again. I don't understand why. Mommy keeps saying the nice vampire man needs to come take my baby brother away, but Daddy says we can't give him away. I agree with Daddy.

Looking down at the baby in the bed with me, I can't imagine ever giving him up. I'm his big brother. Big brothers protect their little brothers. I'll always be there for him. I'll be the bestest big brother ever.

I tuck him in tighter against my side and hope Mommy and Daddy stop fighting so they don't wake him up. Babies need their sleep.

I'm not sure how long we've been asleep, but I hear my door opening. I don't want to get us in trouble, so I keep my eyes closed tight. It's important to be a good boy for Mommy and Daddy.

"He should be in a crib, Esther," Daddy hisses in the dark. "You can't keep pushing the care of an infant off onto our five year old! I'm sorry your sister is gone, but we were blessed with Ethan. It's time to be a fucking mother!"

I feel Daddy's hands brush across my arm as he picks up my baby brother. Daddy is always nice to us both, but he is being really mean to Mommy right now.

"Daddy?" I whisper as he turns to take Ethan out of the room. I don't want my baby brother taken away from me.

He leans down to give me a smooch on my forehead and whispers back, "It's alright, son. Your brother is just moving to his own special bed now in his own room. You can see him again in the morning."

The teddy he places in my arms just doesn't feel right. I should be protecting my baby brother from the nightmares and the yelling. Squeezing the teddy as tightly as I can, I let the tears squeak out of my eyes. It's okay to cry in bed where no one can see. I'm a big boy, but even big boys can't keep everything inside. I'll give this teddy all the love I feel for my baby brother and someday I can give it to him, to protect him when I'm not around...

But I'm always going to be around. It is the job of a big brother, after all.

Fifteen Years Ago

"THREE! TWO! ONE!"

The buzzer goes off and we are officially the champions! This is so freaking awesome!

Looking into the stands, my parents are going crazy along with Alpha Richard and his mate, Miss Anna. Of course, they're all excited... But I can't see Ethan anywhere. Knowing my little brother, he's probably hiding behind the bleachers with a comic book so Mom won't see him. She thinks comics are pedantic or whatever. I'll keep sneaking them to him as much as he wants.

I really want to find him, but Ric and the rest of the team pull me into more celebrations. Little do they know, I completely hate basketball. In fact, I hate almost all of the extra curriculars that my mother makes me do. But it's easier to just go along with her plans for me. If I question her even a little bit, she starts a fight with Dad. I'd rather just pretend to like all of this stuff than deal with more arguments.

When we all pile into the diner for the celebratory ice cream and pizza, I still don't see Ethan. Both of my parents are here, so he should be as well. Where is my brother? The only reason I try so hard at sports is because he always looks at me in my uniform like I hung the moon or something. This championship means nothing without my little sidekick cheering me on.

And that's what he's been for me since the day he was born. He's my sidekick, my other half. He's the only one who understands the pressures put on us to be perfect. I kind of envy him being the younger brother. Mom lets him do whatever he wants when it comes to school and activities. He's so introverted that he gets to just hide in corners and read. I want to do that.

The friendly shoves as we pile into the booths pull me back to the celebrations. I'm sure Ethan is here somewhere hiding from the noise. He doesn't like crowds. I'll find him after we order our food.

"You cool, dude?" Ric asks from my left side. He looks almost as concerned as I am feeling. If there's anyone here who would understand wanting Ethan around for the hero worship, it's my best friend. We grew up together, practically as twins with how often our families spend time with each other. Ric sees Ethan as his little brother just as much as I do, so if anyone gets it, he would.

I lean in to whisper to him, "You seen Ethan tonight?"

He shakes his head, but can't get any words out before my mother is there fawning over the both of us, praising our *undeniable skills* on the court. I swear she will never allow either of us to be viewed as anything less than spectacular. I love my mom, but she needs to take a serious chill pill.

"Mom, where's Ethan?" I interrupt her before she can really embarrass me in front of the rest of the team. "I don't see him anywhere."

She gets that pinched look on her face. I recognize it as her annoyed face. She's not happy that he's not here. Well, join the club, Mom. I ain't happy my little buddy isn't here either.

"He stayed home tonight," she says through clenched teeth. "He was starting to fall behind in his homework, so he had to stay and finish it all."

I watch her walk away while the rest of the guys behind me are still laughing and cheering, replaying all of the awesome moments of the game. My mother goes up to my father and whispers in his ear. When she turns away to go to the other ladies in the pack, Dad looks around frantically before running to Alpha Jameson. Dad grabs him by the arm and drags him out of the diner by force...

"What's that about?" I wonder out loud as I watch the Alpha's face contort in fear while my dad is talking to him. Dad suddenly sucker punches our Alpha, who falls on his ass in the slush of the parking lot. Looking around inside the diner, everyone pretends to not have seen it... everyone except the guy next to me.

"What's he done now?" Ric mutters before turning back to our teammates to continue the celebrations. I watch my dad shift into his copper wolf form and race off toward the pack house. About a minute later, the Alpha follows him.

I wish I had my wolf already. I would follow them. There's no way Ethan is behind in school. The kid is smarter than probably the entire basketball team combined.

———

As soon as Mom stops the car in the driveway, I'm out and racing up to Ethan's room. There's no way he missed my game for homework. Before I can go in, Dad is coming out of the room shaking his head. When he notices me, he sighs and pulls the door closed the rest of the way.

He puts his arm around my shoulders and turns me back toward my room before saying, "Let him sleep it off for a while. He got lost in the woods after school and got a bit scared. He'll be fine by morning..."

I can tell there's more that Dad wants to say, but he sounds like he's on the verge of crying. Dad doesn't cry. I look back over my shoulder at the closed door. What happened to my baby brother in the woods?

"He's going to be fine, Connor," Dad says as he gently pushes me into my room. "I'm going to make sure of it somehow. He's okay for now."

As the door closes behind me, I slide down it to the floor. I don't think my dad meant me to hear that last part. What the hell was in the woods with Ethan tonight?

That settles it. I don't care what my so-called friends think. My baby brother is always going to be allowed to tag along from here on out. I'll never turn him away. There won't be any more getting lost in the woods for him...

I really need to get my wolf soon. Why is thirteen so far away?

Ten Years Ago

As our group piles into the diner, we pretend not to notice the tag-a-long in our midst as usual. I mean, what group of sixteen year olds want to hang out with an eleven year old? Truth be told... I know both Ric and I would prefer hanging out with Ethan over most of the other people here. They're all clinging to us because of our family names. Ric is the Alpha Heir to our pack and I'm next in line for Beta.

Honestly, Ethan and maybe Max are the only ones who don't give a shit about status here. Actually, Max makes fun of our status more than the others suck up to us. It's rather refreshing. I just wish he didn't teach my baby brother to dip his fries in weird stuff. Fries go in ketchup, maybe ranch, but not ice cream... At least it appears that's the only disgusting habit he's passed onto little Blue.

I don't even remember when we started calling him that. Just one day, Ric started calling Ethan little boy Blue and it stuck. He said it's because of Ethan's eyes. Looking at my little brother laughing with Max, I can see the sparkle in those summer sky eyes and have to admit that the nickname is warranted. Although, I kind of have to wonder where he got the eyes from. Neither Mom nor Dad have blue eyes. My eyes are brown. Both of them have shades of brown, although Mom's eyes are closer to a hazel. Maybe our grandmother had blue eyes?

I'm practically gagging watching Ethan drag his cajun dusted fries through his chocolate milkshake, so I turn back toward the conversations happening in the other booth while I wait for Ric to show up after practice. Once he's here, we're all going to go back to the house. At least there, I don't have to suffer from the anxiety of worrying about my brother. He's still such an introvert. I could ease up if he would just make some friends...

"I just don't understand why we have to deal with a toddler freak hanging around," Jessica sneers toward her band of twittering idiots. I'm pretty sure she didn't realize I had turned around. "The little shit does nothing but prevent us from doing actual fun things. How am I supposed to seduce one of them with that *thing* hanging around?"

The giggles from the twits turn my stomach. The only reason I put up with their slutty asses is because the Alpha told Ric and I that we have to treat them nicely. Their families are close or something. I'm pretty sure that just means they're rich. Money or not, my dick is going nowhere near any of them.

Finally, Ric walks in as I'm about to lose my shit over the conversations I'm hearing. I jump up and drag him right back outside so that we can escape the vagina squad. Their only goal lately seems to be to try and trap one of us with sex. Ric is more willing to flirt and play nice than I am. I just want to get as far as possible before they notice we're gone.

As we turn out of the parking lot, I see the rest of the gang start filing out of the diner. Ethan is looking around in confusion... Oh, shit. I left without telling him...

Before I can tell Ric to turn around, I see another little boy run up to my brother and smiles light up both of their faces. I feel my heart do a little flip inside my chest. My baby brother *does* have a friend... but why am I suddenly feeling jealous?

Eight Years Ago

Connie! Help! Come get me, PLEASE!

The voice of my baby brother won't stop. I'm sitting outside the morgue waiting to go in and identify the bodies of my parents and little brother and his voice is screaming in my head. Why the fuck did I let Ric talk me into going to a frat party? Why did I have to promise Ethan pancakes?

If I hadn't promised pancakes, he wouldn't have set an alarm. No alarm means Dad would have caught the gas leak in time. It means I wouldn't be an orphan at the age of eighteen having to look at the charred remains of my entire family...

"You know I'm here for you," Ric says gripping my hand. "You don't have to face this alone."

I can only nod my head. If I open my mouth, I'll start screaming again.

Connie, Please! I'm scared! I wanna come home!

Why won't the voice stop? I'd give anything to bring my little brother back from the dead. I'd give anything to have him play his pranks on me again. I'd even let him shave my head. Just, please don't be my little brother dead on a slab in that room...

"Sinclair?"

I look up to see a guy in scrubs poking his head out of the doorway to the morgue. Ric stands and pulls me up from the bench. My knees feel like jello. I don't want to go in there. The smell already has my wolf on edge. He can recognize the scents of Mom and Dad under the chemicals and smoke and ash. I keep my eyes closed as Ric leads us into the room.

I hear the attendant pull back the sheets covering my parents. I take a look for the benefit of the human in the room, but I know it's them. Turning my head away, I nod. Breathing through my mouth isn't helping and I know I've only got a few minutes before my wolf is going to demand to come out to grieve.

Opening my eyes, I see the smaller shape under another sheet. My wolf is useless after the confirmation that our parents are gone. That lump used to be my little brother...

Connie! Please! It hurts!

The attendant pulls back the sheet and I drop. I think Ric catches me before I hit the floor, but darkness takes over before I'm certain.

I failed him. Thirteen years and the one day I'm not home... I'm so sorry, little brother.

Five Years Ago

Sitting beside Ric, I can't help it. I'm jealous of the fact that he still has his little brother. The well wishers of the pack and surrounding areas are all coming up and offering their condolences, but the two of us are more focused on the toddler sleeping in my best friend's lap. Ric is Alpha now. His parents are dead...

"Such an unfortunate tragedy," another suck-up is talking. "After all of the trouble of moving here to escape what happened with that Ethan boy..."

I can't stop the growl that comes out of me as I jump to my feet. Max is suddenly restraining me and I'm barely holding onto my human form. Glancing at Ric, he's not doing much better, but the commotion wakes Jack up. The screaming toddler catches our attention and we somehow manage to calm down enough to sit again.

It's too soon. It's still too soon. I got another letter last week. I don't even read them anymore. The small flare of hope is just too much. Just because Shaun insists that Ethan is alive doesn't mean he is. It's my fault my little brother is dead. It's my fault our pack had to move away from our ancestral lands.

Shaun is right to blame me. It's my fault his family was expelled from the pack. I asked Alpha Richard to talk to him. I couldn't take the pleading. My wolf wanted to listen to him, but my heart couldn't take it. I don't know what the Alpha said to him, but next thing I know, Shaun and his family were gone. But the letters never stopped. The letters begging for my assistance, begging me to find Ethan and save him...

"Let's get this little guy to bed," Ric mutters, handing a sleeping Jackie to me. "This day was a shit show and I'm ready for it to be over."

I can't help but agree. Looking around at the pack gathered for the wake, I see nothing but crocodile tears. No one is actually mourning the loss of Alpha Richard Jameson. The only person to shed tears for today is Anna, Ric's mother. And her mourners said their pieces quickly and quietly and left us to our grief. These are the leeches... and of course, Jessica is sobbing the loudest of all.

Fuck this pack. I'm here for Ric and for the baby boy in my arms. I failed one little brother. I'm not going to fail this one, too...

2

SHAUN

Twelve Years Ago

"Shaun Eliazor Cleary!"

Ugh, Mom is triple naming me. Does she not understand that it wasn't my fault? I am only eight years old. It's not like I'm a grown up in control of my magic. Jelly Fish... I'm not even supposed to _have_ magic. I'm supposed to be just a werewolf, not a witch.

"You don't get to hide away after freezing the swimming pool with people in it!" her voice echoes through the locker room.

I didn't _mean_ to do it. I told her I didn't want to skip ahead in school. It was bad enough getting picked on in regular classes. Gym class is always worse. I'm smaller than the other kids because I'm at least four years younger than them. They make my life a living hell... Screw it, I'm swearing.

They tried to drown me for goddess' sake. They held me under for so long this time. I don't even know how I'm alive, let alone how I froze the pool. It just happened. One second I was struggling to breathe and the next I'm standing on the diving board and the pool is a giant ice cube. I took off for the locker room at the first scream.

A hand wraps around my arm and yanks me from my hiding place. Before I can even squeak, I feel my mother's magic settling over me, silencing me. I can't argue even if I want to. She rushes through putting clothes on me and drags me out of the room by force. I'm fully prepared to face the principal again, but she surprises me by heading straight for the exit.

"Thanks to your stunt today, we have to leave," she hisses after literally throwing me into the backseat. "This pack only tolerated us because your father said I was his chosen mate and not your birth mother. You went and ruined a good thing, yet again."

It is *not* my fault that we're getting kicked out again. Sure, this is the fourth pack in the last five years, but it's not my fault that I have magic. I didn't ask for it. I was born with it.

Pulling up at our house, I can see that Dad is already packing our stuff into a moving truck. Somehow, every time we have to leave, we're packed up and ready before the Alpha even shows up to give us the spiel.

Every. Single. Time.

"Why is Dad already packing?" I ask Mom as she turns off the car. "There wasn't enough time to go get a truck. I'm not dumb, you know."

She huffs and starts muttering swear words under her breath, climbing out of the car. The slam of her door tells me that I'm still in trouble, but it's not like I wanted to freeze the pool.

I follow her into the house, hoping that Dad hasn't packed up my room yet. I have a few things I want to keep secret. I know I'm only eight, but I know my mind. They'd never accept that I like boys, or pretty things. Seeing the empty boxes in the room, I'm relieved. My secrets are still safe.

"Make it quick, kiddo," Dad calls up from the front door. "We gotta make tracks before the parents get the Alpha Mate riled up. The Alpha already granted us permission to leave and we got a long drive ahead of us."

Picking up my pillow, I dig inside and find my stash of ribbons and lacy doll clothes. Someday I'll be brave enough to find another doll to fit them. Soft and pretty things shouldn't be hidden away.

"Shaun Eliazor! Hurry your ass up!"

Mom's voice makes me jump into action, stuffing my pretties into the bottom of my backpack. It won't take me long to pack up. We've only been here for three months. I barely unpacked from the last time...

Ten Years Ago

Tenth school in five years... Always the new kid.

Now I know what the books about Army brats talk about. But at least the kids in those books make friends or join a sporting team or have cool neighbors that help them fit in. This pack isn't big on the whole neighbor thing. I think the closest house is almost a mile away through the woods.

Mom says this is our last chance for a pack to protect us. She still won't say why we need protection from a pack in the first place. I don't need a roadmap. I may be ten, but I am a genius. She screwed someone over and the only way to hide out is within a pack that doesn't report their members right away. It's why we went from living in Arizona to ending up here in Nowheresville, Ohio.

"Shaun, please introduce yourself to the class," the teacher says, bringing my focus back to the room full of the latest bullies. It's always the same, but at least this time I convinced my parents to only put me one grade ahead of my peers. I'm mostly dealing with kids only a year older. After the last three years of kids three to four years older, it's a welcome change.

"Hello. I'm Shaun Cleary. My family is originally from Arizona, but we move a lot for my dad's job."

I spout off the same lie that I started to use three years ago. It just rolls off the tongue. After a few more awkward moments with the teacher attempting to get a bunch of eleven and twelve year olds to pay attention, I finally get to take my seat at the back of the class-room, next to the window. The kid in front of me hasn't even lifted his head up, but the little red-headed boy next to me jumps a bit when the chair scrapes against the floor.

Ignoring everything around me, I pull out a comic and start to read instead of paying attention. I'd prefer to be reading something more advanced, but I don't want to deal with the beatings today.

"Is that one any good?" whispers the little red-headed boy. "My big brother promised to get that one for me next weekend."

Looking over at him, it's the first time I can remember anyone ever being afraid of me *before* my magic screws things up. But there's fear in his eyes. It doesn't take much for me to put two and two together here. This boy is like me. He's suffering and the adults don't give a crap.

"You can borrow it," I whisper back, handing it over to him. "I've already read it twice."

The shock and joy on his face almost makes me laugh out loud. Has no one ever given him anything?

The bell for lunch rings to signal the end of my reprieve. My neighbor hurriedly places the comic into his backpack and backs himself into the corner behind my desk. He is looking out at the rest of the room while trying to make himself as small as possible... not that it's hard. He should be at least eleven, but I swear he looks like he's seven.

As the rest of the class starts leaving the room, I notice a few of the boys looking around. Even though I know better, I use a bit of my magic to create a mirage wall in front of the boy behind me. None of the guys in this class should be old enough to have a wolf to sense the magic and the teacher seems to be purposely ignoring us all.

"Where's the curse at? Did he run home already?" one of the boys asks while crouching down to look under the desks. "He owes us for making us run after him yesterday. I got yelled at for being all sweaty by my mom. She made me take an extra bath and everything."

I can barely hear the whimper behind me and have to resist the urge to turn around. I need to concentrate to keep my own fear in check and keep the magic under control. I can do small magics like this as long as I can keep my cool...

"New kid!" the jackhole calls out to me making me jump. "You seen the ginger bitch?"

Shaking my head quickly, I pull out my lunch from my bag, making it obvious that I intend to just sit there and keep to myself. I can feel my anxiety rising the longer the other boys are in the room, but I have to force myself to stay in control. We just got here.

I don't want to be the new kid in yet another school if I screw up here...

The bullies file out of the room talking about checking out some other parts of the school. As soon as the door closes behind the last of the other students, I finally take a full breath and drop my head to my desk. That was terrifying. I've been bullied and ganged up on, but it was always out of sight of the teachers and adults. The teacher was there the whole time...

"Thank you," comes the soft voice from behind me. "I'm Ethan. Would you maybe kinda sorta wanna be my friend?"

I've never had a friend before... Maybe this place is going to be like those books after all.

Eight Years Ago

"HE'S NOT DEAD!"

I'm shouting and screaming it to everyone, but no one will listen. The pack was even moved to South Carolina, but it doesn't change the fact that my best friend is NOT dead. He's being hurt every day back in Ohio, but no one will lift a finger to help me find him. I can hear his screams every night. I see what they're doing to him. We *have* to help him, but no one will listen.

Not even Connor... He might have saved me from the Alpha's wrath, but he still doesn't listen to me.

I've had a crush on Ethan's big brother pretty much since we joined the Jameson Pack, but that has died a horrible death. What kind of asshole gives up on his brother like this? It's been less than six months. There's still time to save him from the worst of what is coming. We can save Ethan! Why don't they see that?

"Shaun Eliazor Cleary!"

What the fuck did I do now? I wish that woman would just up and run off like she threatens us with every other day. If the problem that's chasing us is other witches, then she can run from them on her own. I'm tired of running. The only place I'm going to is to find my best friend.

Heading up the stairs towards where her bellow came from, I stagger to realize she's in my room.

SHE IS IN MY ROOM!

I race to the door and my heart hits the floor. My pillow is ripped open, revealing all of my secret stash: the ribbons, the lace, the satin. I upgraded from collecting doll clothes and discovered I like the feel of the soft things on my skin. And now, I'm going to pay for finding an ounce of pleasure outside of her control.

"What the fuck is this shit?" she asks holding up a pair of blue lace boy shorts. "You are entirely too young to be with a woman!"

My heartbeat stutters in my chest. For once, my mother is *not* two steps ahead when it comes to tormenting me, so I play along. If this is how I get out of trouble, I will play it up as much as I can.

"They don't belong to anyone," I tell her. "One of the guys at school made me hold onto them for him. He's giving them to his girlfriend for their anniversary but didn't want his mom to catch him. She doesn't know that he's having sex since he's only fourteen."

The lies roll off my tongue when it comes to my mother. Being a witch, she could probably spot lies if she wanted to, but she doesn't even try. I can't lie to my dad. His wolf can smell a lie a mile away.

So can I, a voice in my head says. I wasn't sure I would get a wolf since I got the magic, but I guess this answers that question. At least I get to find out ahead of time. Ethan never got to talk to his wolf. Only reason I know he shifted on his birthday was a text from him...I've only ever seen his wolf in my dreams.

We will see our friend again, my wolf assures me. I certainly hope so.

My mother suddenly stops gathering up the scraps of lace and satin and I watch in horror as her eyes take on a white film. I know magic when I see it, but this is something different. This is a fated gift of some sort, not active magic. When her eyes clear, they are full of rage and directed at me.

"Now you've done it!" she screams in my face. Throwing the underwear at me, she storms from the room. "We are now officially without a pack, with nowhere to go!"

Seconds later, Dad sends a text to my phone:

Moving truck?

I don't know how he knows, but I text back saying yes. Looks like we're leaving again.

Seven Years Ago

The vampires are forcing us out of the state according to the text I just got from my mother. I can't blame them. The Jameson Pack expelled us. The Heartstone Pack doesn't accept new members without a written recommendation from one of their allies. And according to my mother, I created too many waves with my "imagination" regarding my best friend. We managed to fly under the radar in the neutral human zones, but the vampires found out about us. So now we have to leave again.

Mom still blames me every day for us getting kicked out, but Ethan is not dead. *Someone* needs to go looking for him. I won't stop seeking out help. I will remind Connor that he has a little brother who needs him. I will never stop. I can't stop.

Even though I don't dream of Ethan much anymore, I know he's still out there. He's suffering. I'm just too far away and too young to do anything about it.

"Too young to do anything about what?" a voice comes from behind, making me almost fall in my haste to turn around. What I see makes both me and my wolf almost freeze in shock.

The vampire, and isn't that something, is not much older than I am. At least I don't think he is... But the shocker is that he has an aura about him that reminds me of Ethan. The physical resemblance isn't there, but somehow my wolf and my magic both seem to sense there's a relationship of some sort there...

"You're what... Fourteen?" he asks. "You got your wolf, right? So why too young?"

Looking around the deserted shopping center, I feel the last of my resolve failing. All I'm waiting on is my father to pull up with the moving truck to pick me up. Today is my last hope of getting someone who might be able to help. We're moving to fae territory and will have to stay completely off their radar according to Dad.

The words start tumbling out of my mouth about how my best friend in the whole world was treated like shit by everyone and then abandoned to this horrible fate, but no one believes me. "I just want to save him. I don't care if I ever see him again. I just need him to be saved."

The vampire looks determined as he runs his hands through his black curls. The goth makeup is a bit overkill as a vampire, but even I have to admit he looks good... FOCUS!!!

"Sorry," he mutters. "I'm still getting used to the full power of the vampire glamour thing. My dad says it's no big deal, but my uncle gets all pissy about me not keeping it under wraps... But yeah, I'll go looking for your friend. I need to get away from my uncle for a while anyways and Dad won't let me come home yet."

Before I can say thanks, he is already gone. I'm not sure how long I stare at the spot he disappeared from, but the honk of my dad's truck snaps me out of it. My time is up in South Carolina. Time to go to Atlanta and hide amongst the fae.

One of these days, I'm going to figure out who the fuck my parents pissed off that we have to keep running and hiding...

Three Years Ago

Graduating from med school before even turning eighteen is a feat, right? I don't want to be some Doogie Howser wannabe freak, but it was the only field I could think of where I would always be surrounded by humans so the fae couldn't snatch me away. It was either medicine or drop out...

"Did you hear about any of the internships up near where I'm headed?" my roommate Zach asks while using the vacuum to suck the air from his fourth bag of blankets. The guy collects blankets the same way I collect scraps of lace... ok not scraps, but still.

"I got in one near Charleston and permission from the pack up there to stay while I'm working at the local hospital. They won't make me join," I tell him as I pull out my phone to check for the tenth time on where my parents are.

They basically dropped me off on campus with a notarized letter saying I was allowed to live in the dorm and I have barely seen them since. I took summer classes to stay on campus and Zach took care of me during the holidays. Today will be the first time I actually leave campus without the intention of coming back. A part of me hasn't wanted to leave, just in case Dad comes back for me.

Today will likely be the last time I see my parents, since I won't have any more major milestones for them to come to. Like hell is my mother going to show up at my wedding, if it ever happens. I'm pretty sure she wishes I would just find a good wholesome girl to knock up and settle down with. She only suspects I like dick. I never confirmed it...

Looking at the screen when my phone chimes, I'm disappointed but not surprised to see the message that is there from Dad.

> Congrats Kid!
>
> Super proud dad here. Mom and I can't make it for the ceremony.
>
> Check your email when you get the chance.

Seeing my face, Zach pulls me into a hug. He's like the big brother I never had. I don't understand why, but it makes me miss Connor Sinclair. I don't want to miss that asswipe, even if I imagine it's his body I wrap myself around every night, not my body pillow... He still ignores my letters and emails.

Wiping at my eyes, I force my thoughts away from my parents, my missing best friend, and his brother, to turn them towards the future.

"Let's go graduate and get the fuck out of here!"

One Year Ago

Pulling into a spot near the edge of the parking lot, I stare up at the hospital where I want to work. They have an opening in their obstetrics residency program, and I want it. Babies are easy to deal with. Pregnant moms are hormonal, yeah, but they also don't make me want to blow them up... mainly because of said babies, but still...

Shoving open the door to my beloved Impala, my phone starts to ring. Zach teases me for my Supernatural obsession but Carry on Wayward Son is a great song, especially the cover they found for the last episode.

Speak of the devil...

"Mr. Morrison, elementary teacher extraordinaire! To what do I owe this pleasure?" I belt out while reaching into the backseat for my satchel. "I got an interview in about fifteen minutes at the hospital by you. Want to grab lunch after?"

His chuckle on the other end tells me he was planning on asking me the same question. He's been trying to get me out here since he got hired on full time at the school in the Jameson Pack. I never gave him my full history with the pack, so he doesn't understand why I never come to visit him there.

"Want me to pick you up or meet somewhere?" he asks me. I can hear the papers shuffling in the background. It's spring break time, so I guess he wants a break from whatever assignment he gave to his third graders.

"How long will it take you to get to me here?"

"About forty minutes if I do the speed limit," he laughs in response. Zach is not one who enjoys rules outside of his classroom, although he needs them. "I'll head that way and if you aren't done by the time I get there, I'll drive. If you finish first, we'll meet somewhere."

Shaking my head, I agree and shove my phone into my pocket. As I head into the main doors of the hospital, I have a good feeling about the interview. It almost feels like I'm meant to be here...

Walking into the small café, I spot Zach in the corner. For someone who is the epitome of professional during class times, the parents of his students would have a heart attack if they saw him in his casual attire. Black ripped skinny jeans, spiked hair, guyliner and all. It's like he googled punk and edgy and used the image results to be as basic with it as possible. It's the farthest from his actual personality, but I let him keep his armor.

"No boots today?" His outfit is signature for him with the exception of the shoes. He's wearing athletic shoes in place of his typical black combat boots.

"At the cobbler," he replies before taking a sip of his coffee, if you can even call it that. The amount of sugar this man puts in his drinks...

"Are those sprinkles?" Since when does coffee come with sprinkles?

He gives me a wink and indicates for me to take the seat opposite him. I take off my suit jacket and sit down, glancing quickly at the little menu sealed into the tabletop... basic soups and sandwiches. Works for me.

A server comes over to take my order and says she'll put in Zach's order with mine so they come out together. She just earned herself a great tip. Not many servers are willing to go the extra mile anymore, and it's not their fault. I blame the self entitled pricks who don't understand that a living wage and minimum wage aren't exactly the same thing anymore.

"So?" my former roommate prompts, kicking me under the table to get my attention. "Did ya get it?"

I nod as I thank the server for my super basic salted caramel latte. At least it's not pumpkin spice season yet. I'm totally a basic bitch for the pumpkin spice... Taking a sip, I let the sweet ambrosia fill me up. Black coffee as a doctor is a necessity, but this is how I like to enjoy a cup...

"I'm going to have to fix up the old cabin for somewhere to live, though...if it's even still standing."

My dad sent me a code and an address in an email when I graduated. The address was for a bank and the code was for a safe deposit box at that bank. In the box was the deed to our cabin here in South Carolina. I didn't even know we had owned the old shack. I thought it was a rental with how remote it was.

But I guess it worked out in my favor. This will allow me to live outside of the asshole filled packs around here and still work at the hospital. The only downside to the cabin is how far out it is, so I'll be vulnerable on my own... Well, and no delivery. I got really used to takeout living in the city the last five years or so.

"You know you can stay with me," Zach says when our food is placed on the table. Once the server leaves, he leans over to say a bit more softly, "I'm sure the Alpha will let you crash without having to swear any kind of oath or anything."

I don't even let him get it all out before my head starts shaking. "The Jameson Pack is not the place for me. My family was expelled from that pack. I'm sure I'm blacklisted."

Ignoring Zach's shocked look, I dig in to the food. I probably should have told him about my history with his new pack long before this, but he should be safe there. From what I remember, the Alpha built a veritable fortress against the fae, so I didn't want to ruin this for my friend.

Putting all of my focus onto the food, I make sure that Zach doesn't try to dig. "This turkey club is pretty decent, but the broccoli cheese soup is divine... I need the recipe."

We spend the rest of lunch just catching up. Like always, we end up arguing about the various attempts at spinoffs to our favorite shows and commiserating on the awesome shows that keep getting cancelled before their due time. It's nice having a friend around again, and it hurts a bit to admit how lonely the last two years have been for me.

Leaving the café, I look back on the last couple years since Zach and I split after graduation. Work kept me busy to the point I barely dreamed. No dreams meant no Ethan. It wasn't until I hit the old shopping district that I remembered exactly how long it's been since I thought of him.

The guilt of feeling like I forgot about my best friend still has a grip on me as I pull up to the old cabin in the woods. Climbing out of the car to look at the old death trap, I fight against the memories trying to assault me. My time in this place wasn't exactly happy. Going from a three bedroom house to a one bedroom cabin and having no way to escape my mother's attentions unless Dad drove me into town... I ran into enough doors when Dad wasn't home in the houses. This place was so much worse.

Releasing the tight grip on my magic, I let it soak into the earth at my feet to claim my property. I can't let my anger and sorrow overwhelm me if I'm going to do this right. I need the negative shit to *not* become part of the land. That's how you get haunted shit.

The land recognizes me as the owner and luckily doesn't absorb my bad juju that my memories brought up. It even allows my magic to start to reshape the topography a bit. The driveway is shifted a few feet here, dropped a foot there. The oak trees subtly shift to the left to block the view from the road. Nature is helping me hide.

Reaching out to the edges of my property with my abilities, I can feel some old iron tracks from the old mines about halfway through my property. Those will make a great barrier against the fae...

I allow my magic to manipulate the rails to surround the house. I also manage to shift the iron ore from the rock wall behind the house to completely shield my new home from any fae sight... It should also work for demons, if I ever have the need to hide from them as well.

Of course, they didn't leave any furniture when they left this place behind. *If only my magic understood furniture I wouldn't have to spend money to get anything...*

Time to unpack the car and check out the online marketplaces. I need some cheap furniture pretty quickly if I'm going to avoid coming to the attention of the local packs. At least for the next three years, this is home. Maybe now that I'm back here, I can hold Connor's feet to the fire and get his ass to look into finding Ethan finally...

Who am I kidding? I won't be able to look at him without trying to kill him. My best friend needs to come home, but I'm pretty sure he needs someone living to go bring him back.

3

SHAUN

"Cleary!" A voice shouts from the hallway leading to the Emergency Room intake area.

"I'm a little busy!" I yell back. "Pregnant lady in a car accident trumps whatever you got unless it's two pregnant ladies!"

I see Mick, one of our *special* orderlies come racing around the corner, sliding to a stop next to me as I'm trying to get the fetal heartbeat monitor attached to my patient. She's holding onto the nurse's hand for dear life and I'm not going to do anything to delay finding out how her little one is doing.

"We got one of yours coming in… pretty bad shape from what was called up," he whispers while trying to catch his breath. He is well aware that the humans in the room can't hear what he's saying, but we try to keep it as coded as possible when another supernatural is being brought in. "Can you come, or should I call Savannah down?"

Mick asking about Savannah tells me it's a wolf, not a witch, coming into the ER. That's both better and worse. Better because it means that electronics won't randomly go haywire and cause catastrophic destruction and mayhem in a place that relies on them to keep people alive. Worse because only a stronger wolf or vampire could possibly restrain them if they go nuts.

"They alone or is their guardian with them?" I ask, reaching under the cart to see if the reason I'm not getting anything is because someone forgot to plug the damn equipment in again. I really hope I don't have to leave this frantic mother to be just to babysit some wolf that I either don't know or care to remember.

Savannah is stronger than the average she-wolf, but we don't need a dominance battle if the incoming is close in strength or upset that a she-wolf is stronger. In a less toxic and sexist society, she would easily be a high ranking warrior, maybe even a Beta of a pack. But in the current werewolf hierarchy, she's just another she-wolf. Hell, the female wolves don't even get a designation in most packs... Fucking packs.

Mick cocks his head like he's hearing something no one else can. Odds are he is. I still can't figure out what type of being he is. He scents as human, but he's got some weird abilities that let him be a part of the Supes Squad, as he has dubbed us. I don't question it anymore. Over the last year, he's been a godsend when we need a mediator between the races.

"He's got an alpha with him, but that's the one we're afraid of losing it. The injured one is in bad enough shape, he'll keep until you're done... unless he doesn't make it."

Sighing, I drop my chin to my chest. This boy needs to learn some tact. I often wonder who raised him because of his lack of a brain to mouth filter...

"Have Savannah come down for them and take the moonstone from my locker to put in the room with them. That will help keep things calm," I tell him as I find the loose plug and reattach it. "I'll feel it out when I am done with Mrs. Lockwood here."

I dismiss him as the fluttering sound of the baby's heartbeat comes from the speakers and my patient releases the hold on her tears. The relief in her eyes is what makes all the crazy bullshit worthwhile for me. She's not out of the woods just yet, but at least we've established that her baby is alive.

It takes hours to get the Lockwoods stable and into a room for overnight observation. Six months is a little early for baby Juliette to be making her way into the world. So we're working hard to make sure she stays in and cooks for a bit longer. It's just a precaution, but *I*

24

need to make sure. The fear in Sarah Lockwood's eyes is still haunting me... her eyes are the same shade of blue that Ethan's were... *are...*

Thinking of Ethan reminds me that I should check in on our furry guests. If the patient was as bad as Mick pointed out, there is a good chance that they are still here. I decide I'm only going to do a quick glance in the room, just in case the wolf in question is overly territorial or on edge. It *is* the middle of the night after all and waking a sleeping wolf is never fun...

When I step off the elevator on the floor where we keep our *special* patients, I freeze.

MATE, my wolf roars in my head.

This can't be! I'm not supposed to have a mate! Beings like me are not even supposed to exist, so how in the fuck do I get a mate?

Don't know. Need mate! Claim mate!

Oh, but he really does smell heavenly. He smells like french fries and funnel cake and... My magic starts to rise in response to his scent.

I can't lose control. King Edward only ignores my presence here because my friends keep my secret of being both wolf and witch. He thinks I am only another witch at the hospital. If I lose control, I will lose my life...

The ringing in my head is getting louder and louder...

The lights start to flicker... Shit!

I don't have enough control over my magic right now. I need to leave before I kill someone by accident.

There's no time to wait for the elevator. Racing to the stairs, the door slams open ahead of me. I can't stop. I can't risk everyone in this hospital just to find out who fate decided to saddle with me. Whoever he is, I have to hope he will find me himself, or at least stick around long enough that I can get control and find him later.

Sliding into my baby, I struggle to get her started. My obsession with the show Supernatural made me buy a 1967 Impala, but to afford her, I was forced to get a major fixer upper.

"Please start. Please, baby," I am begging and bargaining with the car while my wolf is howling in my head, trying to overpower the bells roaring with their song. If I don't put some distance between myself and the hospital, I don't know what will happen...

The car finally turns over and I throw it in reverse, narrowly avoiding the brand new Tesla in the row behind me as I peel away from the hospital. I'm going to have to request time off until I can get this reaction under control. As much as I want to be with the one fate has blessed me with, I swore an oath to do no harm...

4

CONNOR

Trying to sleep in a tiny ass recliner in a hospital room is not my idea of a good time. The plan was to have Ric take over so I could let my wolf out for a bit. The anger and guilt and everything are just eating me up inside and I need to release it somehow before some innocent bystander suffers. But of course, my best friend took one look at the bloody mess that was my little brother and he took off. They called him in to keep *me* from losing it, and he ran away... *just like his bitch-ass father*.

I take a few deep breaths to calm myself down. I don't know if it's the breathing exercise or if it's the barely there scent that's been coming and going all day getting stronger. I still can't quite identify exactly what it might be, but it's finally distracting enough that my wolf takes notice of it and stops fighting to come out. I am about to go to the hall to see if I can locate the source when the lights start flickering.

That's the last thing I need to deal with. Right now, Ethan is relying on machines to function in place of his organs while they regrow. His heart already stopped twice on the way here, and I don't think I could handle it happening a third time in my presence. Supposedly a witch on staff is going to swing by to check on us. They provided a moonstone with some calming properties earlier, so I would assume they'd come to collect something so valuable. But so far, only the orderly has been by to check on us since we were brought to this ward...

The lights stop flickering after a moment. I feel the need to find the scent again, but it's gone by the time I get to the hallway. I hear the rumble of an old engine desperately in need of a tune up and head over to the window. If I had a choice in my life, I could be fixing a car like that... an Impala from the looks of it...

I watch the taillights fade into the night and a part of me wishes I had the courage to admit to my Alpha that I don't want to be his Beta. My dream is long dead, though. It died the same night my family did.

A whimper from the bed pulls me to Ethan's side. Looking down at him, I have to remind myself that my whole family did not die that night... The doc said it will likely be days, if not weeks, before he wakes up and is coherent. As long as he wakes up, I can wait forever...

"I'm so sorry, little brother," I whisper as I push the bright red waves away from his face. "I'm so sorry. Shaun was right. I should have listened to your best friend. Please just wake up and I'll give you anything you want..."

Please don't hate me. I hate myself enough for us both...

5

SHAUN

Heading into work for the start of another hell week of five twelves, I wish for the millionth time that I had just taken the seconds needed to find my mate that night in the hospital. It has been months since I scented him, but there is zero indication that he has made an attempt to find me. Rejection sucks donkey balls. I even swallowed my pride and went to the two local packs to look for him last month.

Alpha Heartstone is still a cold hearted bastard, but he granted me access. He even assigned Savannah to escort me through the not so public areas of the pack to see if I could scent my mate.

"Find them and never let them go," he told me gruffly before slamming the door in our faces when Savannah came to collect me from his house.

Savannah shared some of the details with me while we were going around the territory about how her Alpha met and lost his fated mate all before they were both eighteen. That's absolutely fucking tragic. Even though we can't be certain that someone is our mate until after eighteen, the connection is rumored to be unmistakable even without our wolf's acknowledgement. To have lost them and yet never had it confirmed... I wouldn't wish that on anyone.

My heart sank leaving the Heartstone pack without scenting my mate, but it made it necessary to meet up with Zach to see if my mate was a part of the Jameson pack. I got lucky that Alpha Jameson and his top two men were all out of town and the warriors left in charge owed Zach a favor. Otherwise, I would have had to deal with essentially getting tossed out on my ass, I'm sure.

Twin warriors by the names of Seb and Bastian took me around the pack, but that was the limit of my good luck. The only places we didn't go were the Alpha's and Beta's private residences. Seeing as how it was the Alpha who exiled my family and Connor refuses to even acknowledge my emails anymore, I have zero inclination to consider either of those locations for my mate search.

The few people who recognized me as I was being escorted around gave me looks that reminded me why I don't join packs... no one wants to be around the witch boy freak who wears girlie underwear.

The twins were alright though, and since Zach vouched for them, we exchanged numbers. They jokingly said that everyone refers to them as Thing One and Thing Two like in the children's book, but I make it a point to remember to call them by their names. There is power in a name and it should never be forgotten.

Pulling into my usual parking spot at work, I am looking forward to checking in on little Juliette Lockwood. She was born yesterday with no complications, and I just need that win today. My semi-annual email to Connor Sinclair came back undeliverable... I guess he finally got sick of me fighting for his brother. At least the letters haven't come back yet.

Ethan is alive, dammit! Why won't anyone fucking listen?!

I flinch as my windshield cracks when I slam the driver's side door a little too hard. I need better control than this. I'm going to have to request time off to look for Ethan myself and the boss lady won't give me time off if I'm cranky. She's a bit of a sadist...

I finish changing my clothes and am about to head out of the locker room when I notice a text message came through from Seb while I was talking to my boss.

I shove the phone into the holster clipped to my waist and take off for the Emergency Department intake area. I generally don't bother with my white coat if I'm headed to the ER, less laundry disasters after the inevitable mess. I have several pink lab coats now thanks to my red scrubs bleeding in the wash.

Mick comes up beside me keeping pace as I race through the halls, trying to keep my pace to a human acceptable speed. His look is all I need to know it's going to be bad. I may get the prophetic dreams, but Mick has proven to be damn near clairvoyant.

"Level Three S-Trauma," I tell him. "Get me J-packs ONLY."

Mick nods and branches off to start gathering up all of the members of the Jameson pack who are working today. There aren't many considering their Alpha called some sort of mandatory gathering, but I can't have any kind of territorial disputes happening in the hospital because a nurse or orderly caused their packmate pain. I'm glad Savannah is off today because there's no way she would stay out of this, even if I requested it...

The trauma bay comes into view and my magic starts to flare. It hasn't done this since college when I met Zach. Something that will change my life is about to happen and I can't stop it. I can't run from it...

The first SUV pulls up and someone I recognize jumps from the driver's seat to come around to open up the back. Max looks older... more handsome, more rugged. If I didn't know I have a fated mate out there somewhere, I might be tempted to have him pop my cherry... But his scent isn't the one that makes my heart beat faster.

I also recognize Alaric getting out of the back as the two alpha wolves are gently but quickly lifting someone else out of the vehicle. I signal for Mick to bring a gurney up to them. Turning around, I tell my colleagues to take them back and get started. I don't hear a heartbeat from the person they're laying on the bed. I need to focus on the ones my magic can help, and my magic is pulling me toward the brand new truck pulling up next to the abandoned SUV.

Bastian jumps from the driver's seat while Seb jumps out of the backseat of the cab. Before I can even see who it is they are pulling out of the big ass truck, I'm hit with *his* scent - my mate is the one injured.

The bells are back in force and my wolf is struggling to break free. *Need to heal mate! Need to kill who hurt mate!*

My wolf is growling and demanding release. The bells are so loud in my head, I don't even notice Seb is holding me upright. I see his lips moving and it takes me a while to realize he is asking me something.

Pulling energy from the chaos around me, I manage to get enough control to stand upright on my own again. I don't usually like to pull in negative energies, but I need the boost before I completely lose my shit.

"Cleary? You alright?" Seb asks. It must not be the first time he's asked by the tone in his voice. "I need to know you're good to work on the Beta or we need to get someone else down here. Come on, man! Talk to me..."

Seb's anxiety helps me to settle my own. This is crisis mode time. This is where I shine. Shaking myself out physically, I look him in the eye and head toward the trauma room where they are working on... wait a second...

The FUCK did he just say?

Pulling back the curtain, the scent of my mate hits me like a bus. It's every warm and happy memory ever attached to a single unique scent... and the nurses part to allow me to see the one fate has given me.

Connor Fucking Sinclair...

The concussive blast of my magic knocks everyone and everything in the room to the ground. I fucked up and let go of my emotions for one fucking second. Now, none of the electronics work, so the techs and nurses have to scramble to find functioning ones while I stare at the unconscious man in front of me, bleeding out from a gut wound.

Fate has given me to him... the man who insulted me and never believed me. The man who, as of this morning, blocked my emails begging for help. The man who abandoned his thirteen year old brother to hell and torment because it was too hard...

I hope he doesn't make it.

*Do no harm...*my wolf reminds me of the oath I took when I became a doctor.

FUCK!

Taking a breath, I get to work saving his sorry ass. My wolf may be happy about finding our mate, but I will NEVER accept Connor Sinclair as my mate.

6

CONNOR

How in the actual fuck did that bitch get a blade on her?

My abdomen is killing me, but that is to be expected after getting stabbed in the gut. And of course, it happened right in front of my baby brother. Here I was trying to be his cool big brother, to see the hero worship in his eyes again, but I fucked up. All I saw was his fear before...

She had Ethan at knifepoint!

My eyes fly open. I don't have time to waste. I have to get to Ethan. I have to save him!

"Easy, Connor," says a voice to my left. It takes me a few seconds to place it. Seb, or maybe Bastian, is leaning against the doorframe; I haven't committed to remembering which twin is which yet. I haven't seen a point since Max is in charge of them. "You're in the hospital. It was touch and go for a bit."

"Ethan?" I croak out after a few tries. I need to know where my baby brother is. I can't lose him again. I'll never survive it...

"Bossman took him home this morning," he says, but it's not a happy voice. He sounds resigned.

Grabbing the water cup from the table next to my bed, I down some to clear my throat. "Why do you sound not happy about it? My little brother deserves to be home with his family and if he's well enough to go home, that's where he goes."

I might have just woken up, but my wolf is trying to come through. This man should be respecting his Beta. And I say no one has the right to disrespect our boy. He's *mine* to protect... well, mine and Ric's...

The warrior's shoulders slump. I can see the tears in his eyes as he looks up at the ceiling. "Just don't know what good it does to bring a dead body back to the house is all... Kid never had a chance to even meet all of us..."

The water cup falls from my hand and I don't bother to hold back the howl of my wolf in my head...

We failed him again...

There is no future for someone like me.

It's a good thing fate hasn't seen fit to give me a mate. I don't deserve one. I didn't protect Ethan growing up. I abandoned him to that fucking lab, even after hearing his cries for help. I failed to hold onto that bitch because I was trying to impress him... and now he's really truly gone...

Ric will wait for me to be released for the funeral. Once the funeral is over, I'll join my baby brother. I don't deserve to have my life. I'm a worthless excuse for a man and a wolf.

7

CONNOR

"I don't know what is going on with you, Con, but you need to snap the fuck out of it before Christmas hits," Ric says, throwing the tape dispenser at my head. "Your brother is going to have an epic fucking holiday and we don't need your gloomy ass bringing the mood down."

Ducking away from the flying tape, I pour myself another glass of whiskey. Is it wrong to be drinking at noon? Probably. Am I going to stop? Not likely.

"I don't know why you didn't just get the store to wrap everything for you and rent a storage unit," I mutter. I know he hears me. "It's kinda creepy wrapping and storing the presents in the cells where you guys tortured the old pack members that abused and bullied him."

I'm ashamed I wasn't one of the ones to be punished for how Ethan was treated. I mean, no I didn't abuse him directly. But it *was* my fault. He is my little brother. He has always been my responsibility. I should have known. I should have put a stop to it...

He fucking died at least once, that we know of. He was bullied in school. My mother experimented on him in addition to the abuse she and some of the other adults in the pack heaped upon him, both verbal and physical. And yet I did nothing... I knew *nothing*.

I was a selfish, spoiled little prince who didn't even know my own mother was cutting him open regularly for almost a decade. Hell, I didn't even know our basement contained a fucking torture chamber straight out of a horror movie. Meanwhile, I was more worried about how it looked to the girls and guys we went to school with that my little brother tagged along...

I wanted him there. Ric didn't care that he was there. Even Max, once he started hanging on the regular, didn't care. So why did I worry so much about what the others thought?

I abandoned him so much over the years, more than just believing he died that day.... Ric is much better equipped to take care of him...

I need to pull my head out of my ass to at least get through the holidays.

As for Ric, I can't help but chuckle at him digging through the piles of wrapping supplies to find his ringing phone. I recognize the ringtone as Bastian's. Ethan has taken it upon himself to reprogram any phone in reach with designated ringtones for his favorite people. Shaking my head, I sip at the whiskey. Goddess only knows what fresh hell my brother is putting his guards through today. Max still won't walk around the front of a car.

"You better pray to every deity in existence that he is alright, Bas," Ric growls before vaulting over the piles of unwrapped gifts. Throwing the door open, he calls back to me. "Finish wrapping this lot. I need to go to the hospital and find out if I need to kill one of my warriors."

The slam of the front door upstairs breaks me from my frozen state. From what I could make out of the conversation, Ethan is hurt again.

Why? Why is he always the one getting hurt?

Staring at the pile of presents in front of me, I finally let it out. The glittering symbols of joy are the only things in the room to bear witness to my tears and screams, and they suffer for it. So what if I break a few things? I'll replace them. I'm the strong and positive and happy big brother. I'm Ethan's rock. Rocks don't break...

It takes me a while to calm back down after my tantrum. Looking around at the destruction, I can't stop the manic laughter that bubbles out of me. As if it's not bad enough that I ruined his childhood. I'm apparently dead set on ruining the first Christmas he ever gets to have.

I'm so fucking worthless. If it wasn't for the fact that for some reason my baby brother still somehow worships me, I'd be gone. Staying for him is my penance. It's my pain and punishment. Every breakdown. Every flashback. Every single tear that falls from his eyes... I need to be here to bear witness. Each blow to my heart and soul is earned and deserved.

I can only pray that Ethan will find his happiness with Ric in a way that completes him, heals him. I have to have faith that fate got it right with the two of them. I need my baby brother to be happy...

8

SHAUN

> You workin C? Bas is gonna die if you ain't.

I hit pause on my remote as I re-read the message from Seb. I was trying to enjoy my much needed first day off in over two weeks by binging every freaking holiday movie I could get my hands on. They're so cheesy and predictable and mind numbingly sweet that I always find myself hoping that they could be real life. Then again, fate fucked me over with my mate so of course fantasy is the best I can get.

> I'm home. I'll get Sav to meet Bast. I'd never make it in time.

The way the hospital is set up for the S-Traumas aka supernatural beings incoming, there's a liaison to do the intake and to take care of keeping the human staff and patients out until it's reasonable for the patient to be moved upstairs or discharged. Normally, I take care of it, but we got a new doc who is part vamp that is supposed to be on call today. He's an ass and my magic tells me not to trust him. If Seb is looking for me specifically, that means this patient is likely someone important in the pack. That means Doctor Douche is not ideal to be first on scene.

> VIP from Jpack incoming. Keep DD out if at all possible. Msg if u need me to come in.

After sending the message to Savannah, I hit play on my movie. At least someone should be having a happy holiday season, even if it is just some small town girl moving to a big city to fall in love with her new grinchy boss...

> DD is a fucking dead man

I stare at the message that came through while I was in the shower. I don't waste time with texting back, but call my work bestie to get some answers. Savannah doesn't answer, but before I can send her a reply to her message, my phone is vibrating from Mick's call.

"What the fuck happened, Mouse?" I ask as I place the phone on speaker so I can get dressed.

"Well..." he starts sounding super wound up. I swear the boy reminds me of a puppy with how excited he can get. "Doctor Douche is officially on administrative leave pending an investigation and Alaric Jameson's mate is THE coolest dude I've ever met. No offense."

I chuckle as I slide the red and green lace boy shorts up my legs. I love the fact that they make lingerie for men now and that I have the body to pull it off. I've seen stories online about guys who have to special order their stuff to get their junk to fit comfortably and still have it look good. Apparently, my junk is perfectly average enough that they can mass produce my size. Works for me since it saves me money.

"Ric got himself a mate, huh?" I mutter as I close my underwear drawer and slide open my comfort clothing drawer. The snowflake pajama pants have seen better days and are about four inches too short, but they're my favorite holiday time pants to wear around the house. Ethan used to love the snow, so I will pick up anything snow related just to make sure I don't forget about him.

"Yeah, he's the best," Mick blathers on and I tune him out. Ethan will be so crushed to know his pack moved to a place where it hardly ever snows when I find him. I spent over a month scouring Ohio for him back before Thanksgiving only to discover the place he was being held had been destroyed long before I got there. I even checked the old pack lands, but other than a crude dick drawing on a driveway, there was no sign anyone had been there in years.

"So then the Alpha took him back to the pack," Mick finished his story. I didn't hear a damn thing.

"That's great, Mouse. That asshole claiming to be a doctor needs to be fired, but the gods only know what he has on the administration that they keep him on staff," I tell the overly excitable orderly. "I just got out of the bath, so I'm gonna get ready for bed and relax. It's my first off in over two weeks."

"Oh, wow. Super duper sorry, Shaun. Get some rest. We'll gossip laters," Mick says before the line cuts out. I don't mind the sudden cutoff in our conversation. The only thing on my mind right now is Ethan and finding him. I want to bring him home for Christmas. He never had a Christmas, not really.

Santa, if you were ever real, bring my best friend back to me. Bring my family back to me.

9

CONNOR

I can't believe Ric! How in the hell did he screw up so badly that my baby brother is now beyond my reach? As if it's not terrifying enough to find out that Ethan is the grandson of the fucking Vampire King... and we all realize that is the ONLY reason people are not dead for the mess those fucking betas made... Now, he's taken sanctuary in the Heartstone pack because his stupid fucking mate can't control his fucking temper!

> Please tell me you know of a way for me to reach my brother

I send the text to Max hoping that he has an answer. He cares about Ethan just as much as we do. If fate hadn't put my brother with Ric, I would be positive he belongs to Max. The man has done nothing but show loyalty to my brother, even above his Alpha and Beta. He even knows so much more about my baby brother than the rest of us...

> I'll talk to him and get back to you. It's up to LD if he wants to see you.

I read back the message for what seems like hours. It would serve me right if Ethan finally decides to cut me out of his life. I don't know if it's my imagination or a dream, but I can almost hear another voice in my head.

You are better than this, sweet boy.

The ping of a new text stops my mind from spiraling on that new voice.

University Café. One hour. Only you.

I jump in my Tesla to head toward the University in the Heartstone pack. That is the place where Ethan takes his classes, so it makes sense to have it be the meeting location. It's technically considered neutral even though it is run by the Heartstone pack. Knowing that Ethan should be on a break from class for another two hours means I will have about an hour with him if I hurry.

Pulling into the visitor lot of the campus, I run to the café. I refuse to waste a single second with my baby brother. As I pull open the door, I see him and Max sitting with a woman I recognize as a nurse from the hospital. Ethan's face lights up when he sees me. I smile on reflex, but I can't help feeling like absolute shit for it. Why did it take me almost a month to figure out he didn't plan to come home? That he was in another pack this whole time, avoiding all of us?

I know he doesn't blame me for anything, but it's all my fault. I should have known something was wrong that night after the warehouse. I should have woken up faster when he reached out to me that morning. I should have found him before he fully left the territory...

Before my self-loathing gets too out of control, I am almost knocked over by the enthusiastic hug I receive from the little ginger boy who has attached himself like a barnacle to me. It's been almost twenty years since he has latched onto me like this...

"I'm sorry I left Kun-Kun," he mutters into my shirt. "I had to save you all. Daddy was mad. I don't want to make him mad anymore. Jackie needs Daddy to be happy."

I raise my eyes to the ceiling as I struggle to contain the growl his words are invoking. My wolf and I agree wholeheartedly that our

Alpha fucked up big time by losing his temper. I look over at Max and Savannah and the two of them look like they're fighting the same battle I am. The only thing I can think of to keep my cool is to hold onto my baby brother a little bit tighter.

"Ric wasn't mad at you," I whisper into his curls. "He was mad you were trying to take the blame for something that is *absolutely* NOT your fault. It is not your place to fix other people's mistakes."

Before I can say anything else, he starts shaking his head vehemently and backs away. I can see the tears forming in his eyes, so I do the cowardly thing and change the subject.

"Enough about the jackass," I spit out before his emotions take over and feel pure relief at the watery giggle that comes from Ethan. "How are classes going? Where are you staying?"

We spend the next hour just talking. As if the vampire revelation isn't enough, now I find out that Alpha Bennet Heartstone is his birth father. As much as it stings that I'm not his only family anymore, he's got a network of strong protectors in his father and his grandfather now that they know he exists.

I can start falling back. He's safe now. He's loved.

I'll fade away slowly so that it's not a shock to him when I'm gone. He doesn't need me anymore.

I can't help but squeeze him a little tighter for our hug goodbye when he goes off to his next class. I love our little boy Blue, but he is better off without me. I stay in the café long after Ethan and the others have left.

My phone pings with a message as I sip my now tepid coffee.

> YRU acting like this is the last time UR seeing him?

> I WILL kill U if U abandon him like Ric has

I have to smile at the messages from Max. He has always been observant, but he doesn't understand. He won't have to kill me. My baby brother is the only thing I have left to live for. My life is his, now and always.

10

SHAUN

Motherfucking fae in MY hospital.

I can't deal with this today. Bad enough I felt that rush of jealousy and emotion out of the blue today, but then I had to spend most of my day dodging their faerie magic searching the building for someone.

They showed some sort of official document to the boss lady and she allowed them to magically read every wolf on the premises... except me. I got a clause put into my contract when I was hired that no one can subject me to any magical testing without my express permission. The technical reasoning is why on my official documents has me listed as witch. Only the boss lady and a few others know I'm *both* wolf and witch. The true reason is because magic used on me without my knowledge can have literal explosive consequences...

While the two faeries are waiting by the front doors for the next shift to come in, I decide to slip out the back. Mick seems to be the only one of us on the Supes Squad willing to be anywhere near them. The fae seemed interested in him until they did their reading. Dunno why he has abilities, but he apparently comes off as pure human to them as well. It used to bother me, until he told me his uncle dabbles in weird cult like shit, trying to get magic to work for him. Mick thinks his stuff is a side effect of living in the same house.

Mick gives me a wink as he takes another swig of his energy drink and manages to block the view to the door. Taking advantage of his diversion tactic, I successfully reach the outside without being noticed. The fresh air is wonderful after the antiseptic stench of the hospital. Plus, it doesn't hurt that the weather today is pretty amazing for early March. I can almost imagine rolling the windows down in the Impala and cruising through the mountains...

I have to imagine it since I can't seem to get the driver's side window down more than a couple of inches.

Speak of the Impala... who the FUCK is touching my car?!

Storming over to the car, I yell at the guy who dared to put his hands on my beloved...

He looks kind of familiar and... Hold the fuck up!

"Ethan?!"

He looks confused for a second and then I see him light up. I race toward the man, tackling him into a hug. Holy fucking shitballs! He's here!

He's still fucking tiny, but he is really here in front of me. I wondered why the dreams stopped. I didn't want to think the worst, but the thought was there... It doesn't matter anymore. He's here and he's alive.

I'm only half following the conversation when he mentions someone calling him from the hospital about Jack Jameson. That snaps me fully back to awareness and I inform him that no one from the Jameson pack has been brought into the hospital at all. I've been on for about twenty hours at this point, so I usher him into the car to continue talking.

He mentions some Felix guy. I don't know a Felix, but I do know that there are some people in admin that I haven't met. One of them might be this Felix, but then it hits me. It's the fucking fae.

My wolf snarls as we scent them. They are outside of the hospital, now. There is no reason for them to be outside if they are looking for a wolf who works there, but they are looking for Ethan.

Was it the fae that took and held him all this time?

Fuck that shit! They don't get to have him back.

I pull out and race toward home, the only place in the entire county fully guarded against the fae. My best friend is back and I'm not losing him again. Now that I'm an adult and have the skills necessary, I'll protect him since no one else ever did.

11

SHAUN

Staring at the sleeping form of my best friend, I realize I'm out of my depth. Not only does he have severe PTSD from his time in captivity, but he's also pregnant with twins. There's no denying that Alaric Jameson is his true and fated mate, but why the fuck is a pregnant omega running around on his own, nevermind he's the fucking Alpha Mate.

Is it wrong that I kind of always hoped my bestie would end up with Max instead?

I know my BFF has been head over heels for the Alpha Heir, well now Alpha, for pretty much his entire life, but the guy has always been a self-centered prick. At least Max really saw Ethan back then. He didn't notice me most of the time, but he zeroed in on my best friend.

Ethan's whimper shakes me out of my memories, only to be thrown into his. This is new...

"Why the fuck is she pregnant, Janice?" Mom is mad at the maid lady from the Alpha's house. I don't know how Janice is somehow in control of whether or not someone gets pregnant, but apparently Mom thinks she can control it.

"It's bad enough she gave him Alaric. There can't be another one!" she shouts into the phone.

I think she's forgotten I'm here. That's the way I prefer it. But her being already mad means there's no way I can get out to the pond to meet Shaun on time. I hope he doesn't think I'm blowing him off today.

Sneaking back upstairs to Connie's room, I hope he still hasn't fixed the broken latch on his window. If I sneak out this way, I'll need it to come back in. The windows in my room are sealed permanently shut, so I can't get out there.

"Fucking fix it, Janice! Or it's your child next. You have the tea. Make sure she drinks it."

Is it wrong to be happy to hear her threatening another kid? Maybe if she has someone else to focus on, I can live like a normal kid for once...

I'm barely over the threshold of Connor's room when she calls for me.

"You little abomination! Get to the basement, NOW!"

If only I had my wolf with me. My birthday is next month. If I don't get my wolf, I don't know what to do. She might actually kill me if I don't have a wolf...

"NOW!"

I jump and run down the stairs to the basement. Glancing at the clock, I realize I missed our meetup. I hope Shaun can forgive me...

My ass hits the hardwood floor as I literally fall out of Ethan's memory. That was an extremely strange experience. Never have I ever "become" the person whose memory I'm witnessing. I've also never had my magic pull me into a memory without me actively doing the spell for it.

Was it even my magic that did it? Ethan does have his whole mind speak thing going for him now. Maybe he has something with memories as well? I'll have to ask him when he wakes up... if he even wants to talk to me again.

Climbing back to my feet, I head into the living room to boot up my old laptop. I have some brushing up to do on omega pregnancies. I know they were a footnote in my classes, but that was years ago and not nearly detailed enough.

12

CONNOR

Pulling into my garage, I feel lighter than I have since Christmas morning. As the bay door lowers behind me, I stare at my present from Ethan and can't wait to take it out for a long ride. Only a kid who has yet to learn the value of money would think a Ducati would be a reasonable present. I can't stop the chuckle that rises up in my throat as I turn to head inside the house.

Even though I just had coffee a few hours ago with Ethan and Max, I decide another cup is in order. Ever since Ethan allowed me to meet him that first time in the café, I think I can actually accomplish something with my job in the pack. Not talking to my baby brother for a month while he was hiding away really did a number on my mental health and I let my pack responsibilities suffer. Well, that ends now...

Taking my cup to the office in my otherwise empty house, I wipe the dust off the top of the laptop and open it to get to work. Now that Ethan's taken care of, I can focus...

Barely ten minutes into my newly productive mindset, my phone rings with Ric's tone. As much as I don't want to stop my momentum, I still need to answer my Alpha... even if he is the biggest asshat on the planet for driving Ethan away.

"Make it quick, asshole. I'm on a roll with the financials and don't want to stop," I tell him as I put the phone on speaker to keep working.

"When did you leave Ethan?" he asks me in a rush.

"Dude, I'm not helping you make up. You were an ass and you need to do your own fucking groveling." I'm not taking his side over my baby bro's. Never gonna happen.

There's a pause and I can hear Ric taking some deep breaths on the other side. "I got a letter today."

I don't understand why the Alpha getting a letter has anything to do with Ethan, but I stop typing and give the phone my full attention.

"It was an official notice from the fae trying to lay claim to Ethan. Can you get in touch with Heartstone to check on him? He won't answer me."

I freeze. The fae want my brother? This can't be happening. This isn't happening...

"Connor? Dude! CONNOR! Answer me!"

I can't answer. I can't breathe. My wolf is struggling to break through, but I can't let him. He can't help. I need hands and fingers and to talk to check in with Ethan, but my wolf isn't listening to me.

I can still hear Ric on the phone as my wolf crashes through the window to runs out into the forest. The all consuming thought running through my mind is to find our baby boy before they find him. I can't have lost him already. I can't... I won't survive it.

13

SHAUN

I've barely cracked open my old notes when I feel someone trying to invade my mind. The feeling is similar to the one I get with Ethan speaking in my head, so I'm pretty sure this is someone he is related to. My money would be on his grandfather. The magic of it smells kind of close to the vampire that helped me out years ago, so I open up enough for the intruder to speak to me.

What do you want and why are you violating my mind like this? I send back to the intruder.

I can feel their surprise at my ability to control the flow of information. I don't scent as a witch thanks to my wolf side, so most other supernaturals don't recognize what I am unless I reveal myself.

Plus, I long ago mastered the technique of copying magics used against me. I got the idea from an anime, and managed to mold my magic to work the same way the character's magical eye did. I might not be a ninja, but I'm not a regular witch.

I am Edward, vampire king of this region. You are with my grandson, are you not?

I can't help but chuckle at how much Gramps here is trying to pull his weight. He did nothing for me when he kicked my family out of our home. He never protected me when I was a fucking child abandoned in the heart of the fae territory and subsequently hunted every time I set foot off campus. He never even helped find Ethan, his own fucking grandson. Some king he is. This asshole gets nothing from me.

Yeah I'm with him and he's safer with me than he is with any of you. I know who you are and who you're with. They don't deserve him. None of you do.

My magic starts to rise with my anger, so I let it direct itself to the vampire and put power to the next part.

Those asshats don't know a fucking thing about him or me. When they remember my name, then you'll be able to find him. If they don't remember me, you'll never locate him until HE decides you can.

Cutting off the link to the vampire, I try to get back into my research, but it's only a few minutes later when my magic connects to my phone and dials a number I have never seen before. I am honestly surprised one of them remembered me so quickly. My money is on Max, even though I hope it's Connor who picks up. I want him to be the one to remember me.

The call is declined.

What the actual fuck?

So they remember me, but don't want to find Ethan?

My magic pulses through the phone once again.

Declined.

This is fucking ridiculous! They truly don't deserve him. I'll gladly keep my bestie with me forever if they keep this up.

My magic pushes the call through one final time. If they don't answer, I'm done. I'm not forcing this reunion if they don't want it.

"You remembered my name?" I ask when the call connects even though I know that's the only way my magic would have attempted the call.

"You're the brat who tried to help him back then, aren't you?" Max asks. "Shaun, right?"

"I never thought you were as dumb as you looked, Maxi-pad." I chuckle a bit at the familiarity of the exchange. It's like the last nine years disappeared and I've got the pseudo big brother teasing me again.

I rub my chest at the phantom pain of knowing it wasn't Connor who remembered me, but this isn't about me.

"Who were the kids on the bikes?" another voice breaks in. It takes me a second to recognize the voice as that belonging to Alaric Jameson.

"Bikes?"

"The bikes, when Ethan busted his rim, around his tenth birthday or so..." he prompts.

"Oh that time?" It takes me a second to remember even though he was closer to eleven or twelve at the time. I'm not sure what this has to do with anything, but I see no harm in telling him. "Yeah it was Timmy Donovan, Justin O'Keefe, and Sidney Black that ran him off the trail. I tried to catch up in time to stop them, but my bike popped the chain. I got there as quick as I could once I saw them riding away."

I can *feel* the self-deprecation through the phone. Ric is seriously making this all about him and his fucking failures instead of focusing on his fucking mate - his *pregnant* mate.

His lack of panic makes me realize he doesn't even know Ethan is pregnant. What in the fucking hell is wrong with this fucking pack?

"You aren't a bad person for having a good life, douchebag," I snarl into the phone. "You're not even a bad person for not listening to a kid screaming that his best friend was alive. You were so lost in your own grief you lost sight of everything but *your* best friend. It makes me wonder which Sinclair you actually wanted for your mate."

I can feel the exact moment when Ric realizes exactly who he's on the phone with.

Took him long enough.

It's not like I spent every fucking second that I could with Ethan in their pack. Meanwhile, Ethan wanted nothing more than to be around his big brother and the Alpha Heir. Therefore, I spent more time with them than I ever wanted. Trying to keep a low profile while hanging around the future leaders of the pack isn't a smart plan, and my mother never hesitated to point that out.

"Yeah, you figured it out didn't you, RRRRRic?," I say over the line. "I told you all he wasn't dead, but no one listened. For years, I said it but NONE of you listened. I went looking for help to find him and NONE OF YOU LISTENED!"

There's silence on the other side, but I continue on. My magic is rising uncontrollably, and I don't want to stop it. I pour it through the phone so they will all feel the true impact of their actions over the years. They need to know how they failed him. They *NEED* to feel the pain I felt every single time they didn't take action.

"The Jameson pack abandoned him completely, leaving the state when he was just an hour away, praying daily for someone to set him free from that place, one way or another.

"The Heartstone pack told me that they didn't meddle in death investigations and that I should *get therapy* to get over the death of my friend."

There's a whimper on the other end of a wolf I don't know, but I can only assume it belongs to Ethan's sperm donor, the wolf who abandoned his own son just because he couldn't be bothered to listen to me when I was a teenager looking for help.

Good. He deserves to feel the pain of regret. He abandoned a child to literal torture for years. Regardless of the blood ties, no child in danger should be ignored that way.

"His vampire sire *felt the blood song,* but did nothing to locate him except feel guilty and call it a dead end when his only lead drove off a cliff."

I *feel* the pain those words inflict on the vampire. There's more guilt tied up in that statement than just dealing with Ethan, but I don't have time to unpack things that don't concern me.

The magic is in control and drives me to continue.

"The only person who listened and helped was a *sixteen*-year-old vampire who didn't want to be the next king. Another child was the only one to care. He jumped at the chance to help someone who really needed it. And for his trouble, he spent years in that hell himself."

This news seems to strike pain in more than just the vampire king. Unexpectedly, I feel excruciating sorrow from Max. He is probably the only one on the other end of this call that I don't want to feel the pain right now.

Knowing I hurt someone who did nothing to deserve it, I try to pull back some of the magic, but it's still surging forward stronger than I would prefer, than I can control without assistance. I start yanking open drawers in the kitchen to find something I can use to siphon the excess away while I continue talking.

"But placing the blame for what happened falls to *all* of us and yet none of us at the same time," I grind out through clenched teeth.

It shouldn't be this difficult to reign in my magic...

"The real culprit in all of the things that happened to him is Esther Sinclair, but she's dead. From her, we can move on to Richard Jameson, but again - dead. Then there's Carl Welling, yet again dead.

"Every person who *truly* wronged him is dead," I push as much of my magic into these words as I can to get it under control again. I can see the flaring of my aura as my magic turns my next words into a full prophecy.

"Karma and the fates will decide who has wronged him and they will mete out their punishment and their punishment shall be death."

My power, having served its purpose, fades into the background once again. I haven't lost control of my abilities since I was ten. At that time, my abilities were dangerous enough. Now? They would be catastrophic. I can't afford to lose control again...

"Ok now that that's done," I fake a chipper tone. I'm still physically shaking from the adrenaline. "How do you wanna handle this fae shit going on, cuz I can keep him here and he'll be safe but I doubt he's gonna wanna stay once he wakes back up."

"Why wouldn't he want to stay?" Ric asks at the same time the other Alpha asks "How can you keep him safe?"

"Alpha Heartstone, puh-lease!" I say. "I'm a witch and a wolf and a genius. Plus, I've been running from the fae pretty much since Alpha Dick kicked me out of the Jameson pack and my parents abandoned me in the heart of Atlanta.

"My house is hidden by iron, steel, and oak. The cliff at the back of my house has iron ore running through the rocks and the overhang blocks the sight of my house from above. My drive is invisible due to proper terrain development and the oaks protect my home from the view of those who would do me or my guests harm."

Alright, I might be getting a little too cocky here. I should probably tone it down. These are all alpha men after all. Since they are important to my best friend, I'm going to try to make nice with them for his sake.

"There are old rail tracks from the iron mines that run along the perimeter of my property and I *may* have manipulated them a bit to completely seal my property from the fae."

Rolling my shoulders, I pull back the curtain on the window to glance outside. I appear to be entering the next phase of my adrenaline crash... paranoia.

Is it paranoia if we smell the fae on the wind? my wolf asks, setting my own hackles back up. It's bad enough the alarm for my warding has already been triggered once in the last day. I haven't even had a chance to go out and reset that one, so the vulnerability is grating on me even more.

"Oh, and don't forget I'm a witch, so I have placed spells to keep out trespassers and intruders and any beings with malicious intent ... and people I just don't like... you know, the usual."

I add on a chuckle full of false bravado, knowing that not a single one of them will hear the fear under it all. I reach out to my wards and find that about ninety percent of them are still up and active. Whatever triggered the alarm earlier must have run off.

"Sounds like the safest place for him," Max says, sounding like his old self again. "What's the issue?"

"See, I thought he knew and I didn't know about him having PTSD and everything," I say and before I can get to the point of my sentence, growls are coming from everyone on the other side of the call.

"RELAX!" I say to cut them off. *Fucking alphas!* "I'm not judging him for having PTSD. It's only natural considering what he's gone through... although the no therapy thing is something I do have an issue with but that's just because I'm a doctor myself..."

Way to bury the lead, dumbass... at least someone on the other end recognizes my word vomit.

"I understand why you think he won't stay there with you," Ric breaks in, apparently catching on quicker than the others. I didn't know the prick had it in him. "Would you be willing to stay somewhere else and allow Ethan to stay there with say, Max? or even Connor? I know *I'm* not welcome..."

Well, that's a surprise. I've never known a wolf to voluntarily stay away from their mate, especially an Alpha. I can't say I like the fact that he is staying away from his pregnant mate. It goes against nature.

Since when do you have an issue with that?

Damn wolf snickering in my head. He needs to keep his trap shut.

"I'd let you in long before I'd ever grant access to that piece of shit Connor," I snarl in response to the thought of my sorry excuse for a mate showing up. "Max can come, and the vampire that helped... no others will find my house so send no one else unless you want to lose them in the woods."

My energy is flagging. I need to get some sleep soon for myself or we are going to have some really big problems. I don't have anyone or anything to pull from out here without endangering us both. I can't pull from the land or the wards, and I won't pull from Ethan. Sleep is my only option...

My finger is just above the screen to disconnect the call when Ric's voice breaks in. I jumble my phone, but hear him ask, "Shaun? Can I get one more favor from you?"

"This is for Ethan, not for you," I grumble as I save the device from meeting the hardwood. I really don't need a broken phone on top of everything else. "If it wasn't for the fact that he won't stay in this house if I'm here, I'd have let you stew in the knowledge that he was outside of the precious pack protection you guys all seem to believe is flawless."

"Ethan would want Jackie safe," Ric rushes to say.

14

SHAUN

Max and Jack are finally settled in at the cabin, and I'm so fucking exhausted. Between my research and the emotional backlash from my pregnant omega best friend and keeping my magic from killing everyone in a ten mile radius, I'm zonked. I *really* need to find time to get some sleep in here soon or my grasp on the magic inside me is going to become even more frayed.

As for the kid that showed up with Max, Jack is an absolute treasure. Considering I think Ric is a total asshole, he did something right with raising this kid... Then again, he could have hired nannies if he wanted. I haven't been around enough to be able to make any real assessments, but Jackie seems to love his big brother for some reason. In deference to the kid's viewpoint, I think I can give him a *bit* of a benefit of the doubt.

Wow... even my thoughts are rambling at this point...

Max is in the bedroom, dealing with Ethan's emotions after receiving the gift of Mr. Whiskers from the big lug. Jack seems to be content at my sad excuse for a table with what looks like his homework. I'm gonna have to ask Zach to go easy on the kids. That is a lot of homework for an eight year old...

I jerk awake as my anti-fae alarm goes off again. My magic is telling me this isn't the same as last night. Whoever broke through my wards is approaching the cabin, and fast. I snatch up my shotgun filled with iron pellets and take up my stance in the window. Fucking fae... I'm surprised they're even willing to try.

I hope it fucking hurt to break through my wards.

I send my magic out to repel anyone meaning harm, but all I get back in response is an overwhelming feeling of guilt... whoever this is, they don't want to hurt us... Shit... Why do I feel bad, now?

You care, my wolf chimes in. *Doctor means you care.*

Grumbling to myself, mostly upset that my wolf is more rested than I am, I open the door to find a beautiful fae woman on the porch. She can't enter unless I grant her entry, but she hasn't even tried. The look on her face is serene, but I can see the pinch of pain around her eyes. She didn't get through my wards unscathed...

"Who are you and for what reason have you breached my wards and suffered the pain to come here?" I ask, feeling an echo of the pain she felt crossing the iron and spells. The physical pain isn't bothering her as much as the memory spell. I didn't expect a fae to feel remorse or regret, but damn, that one hit her hard.

She looks me in the eyes and tells me her name is Celeste and she came to warn and protect Ethan from one of the fae princes who wants to take him. She feels genuine to me and my magic hasn't attacked her, but I need to make sure of her intentions before I invite her inside...

"Why would you come here, risk the pain inflicted by my wards to protect Ethan?" I know she sensed the spells and the iron and knew exactly what would happen. She scanned me magically as soon as I stepped onto the porch, the same way I did her. She has more than enough ability to sense the gigantic *KEEP OUT* signs that my magic would be to anyone with even a smidge of witch or fae blood in them.

Her eyes are haunted when she finally answers. "He saved me many times over, both physically and mentally. I can never repay the debt, but I must try as our bonds demand it. You will get no details, but if you know even an inkling of what he suffered, you should be aware that much of it was to protect myself and others from suffering the same..."

Her eyes take on a glassy sheen as she whispers, "He made himself their target. He was just a child and he protected us all..."

I stare unabashedly as a single tear rolls down her cheek before she shakes herself out of the memories. There is no reason to keep her outside now. I don't know all of the details, but she is most definitely not someone I have to worry about hurting any of the people currently under my roof.

Once inside, I call out to Ethan to come to the living room. He needs to come see his old friend, even if it is just so that he gets the knowledge that he made an impact with someone besides me... Their reunion is something to see, even with the iron burns she received from his hidden blade in Mr. Whiskers.

Who would have ever thought I would have a fae in my home voluntarily? This life is so weird...

After some tea and discussion, Ethan is overwhelmed. Turns out Celeste's brother is an idiot and the damn fae prince wants Ethan because Alpha Dick promised him to them like ten years ago or something. That man was a fucking twatwaffle who should have never been in a position of power...

While Ethan heads to the bedroom to think, I busy myself with making another round of tea for myself and Celeste. For a fae chick, she's really not that bad. Of course, she says she and her brother are halflings so maybe that's why my magic isn't going haywire with her. Then again, it could also be the sleep deprivation and caffeine overhaul making my instincts completely unreliable that makes me want to be friends with a fucking faerie.

Max's phone rings and I hear him answer while I'm pouring out a fresh cup for myself. I assume the caller is Ric by the way the warrior answers the phone but when it becomes immediately apparent this isn't a social call, I set the kettle down to pay attention. The Alpha's voice on the other side of the call is frantic and Max rushes to the bedroom only to let out a loud "FUCK!"

Celeste and I both follow Max into the room, only to see him become a pure white wolf and dive out the open window... Why is the window open?

The fae woman picks up the phone and continues to talk to Ric while I rush to the bed to check on Jackie. There's no way a faerie could have gotten inside without me knowing, right? Oh, fuck. How badly did I screw up?

Luckily, the boy seems fine... just really confused by the action going on around him. He had been taking a nap peacefully up until about two minutes ago.

I finally clue myself back into the conversation when I hear Celeste asking if Ethan will fight back. I can't hold back the laughter. Dark humor has always been my go to for stress. One can't afford to be afraid around the fae...it makes it hurt worse...

"Oh, he'll fight back," I say as grab the shotgun from the hall and cock it. "His temper, once activated, is unrivaled."

I move to stand by the window and push my exhausted magic to seek out the breaks my warding to figure out how in the hell another fae got past them. The physical pain of crossing the iron should have been enough to incapacitate them, but somehow there was one strong enough to carry him off afterwards?

After my scan, I relax my grip on the gun. There are no cracks or breaks in the warding on the cabin itself. Ethan must have gone outside the house, otherwise there was absolutely zero chance of him getting grabbed. If it was Celeste's brother, being a halfling and all, he might not have registered to my wards as a fae...maybe that's how? Shit, I need to keep my cool...

Take charge. Take control. This is where I thrive...

"...does he have Stabby?..."

I'm still half listening to the phone conversation, so I glance around the room. My eyes land on the chair in the corner where my spare blankets are usually piled up. In their place, is the ratty old teddy bear... the one that hides Ethan's secret switchblade.

"Mr. Whiskers is here..." I mumble in defeat. My best friend was stolen from right under my nose and there's nothing I can do. I'm no better than the rest of them....

15

CONNOR

"What the fuck, Ric?!" I scream at my Alpha. "Last I heard, he was safe with a friend in a fae-proof house! What happened?"

Ric glances over at me as he drives us further into the mountains on the winding road. He is just as tense as I am. I am still pissed off that they all felt it was a good idea to leave Ethan with a wolf that none of us has seen or talked to for over eight years. I mean, yeah... I liked Shaun as a kid. But as an adult? How do we know he isn't holding a grudge against us? He has every reason to hate all of us for not listening to him...

Not hate. Never hate, my wolf whimpers in my head. The animal has been all sullen and moody for the last six months or so, but I need him to be angry along with me. It doesn't matter that deep down I know Shaun would never hurt Ethan. I need the anger to not break into a million pieces...

"Max was in the house with him. And there is quite possibly no other place in the damn state warded that strongly against the fae," he tells me as he pulls off the road into what I swear a second ago was just forest. "The fae got access to the university, the hospital, and *our pack.* Dude, they even made it to the elementary school."

Ric glances over at me and I know exactly what he feels. They almost took Jack...

"Ethan was safe as long as he stayed inside the house. He must have gone outside, but we'll get him back... *we have to...*"

While Ric maneuvers his way through the trees on a path I can't see, I take a chance and try to see through Ethan's eyes. I promised my baby brother not to use this ability on him unless it was an emergency due to the headaches it can cause, but I'm pretty sure it qualifies. I'll buy him some ice cream to make up for it.

I let the power wash over me and my own vision goes dark. I close my eyes, giving up on the sight side of things and try to listen in. All I can hear is the sound of a car moving quickly on a road. I can only assume they're traveling on a highway or interstate... but that doesn't help me. The radio is playing some pop music from when I was a kid and whoever is in the car with Ethan is singing along softly.

"If you're done doing your freaky senses takeover thing, we're here," Ric says, pulling me back to myself. "I'm not sure how the kid is going to react to you being here, but he didn't say not to bring you this time. But if anyone other than me wants Ethan safe, it's you."

I climb out of the car and get hit with an incredible scent before it dissipates immediately. It tickles a memory... My wolf is wagging his tail inside of me, but I feel only confusion and frustration at his antics. How can he be happy when our boy is kidnapped?

Looking up at the porch, I clench my jaw to keep it from falling open. The scrawny little kid that ran around with my brother grew into a fucking unbelievably gorgeous man. He's only an inch or two shorter than myself, but the lean muscles I can make out underneath his t-shirt shows me that he definitely is not the same boy I knew.

My wolf is sitting up and taking notice, getting more and more excited, while another part of me starts sitting up as well...

That's... unexpected. My dick hasn't gotten up for anything since the day my family died... well, my parents anyways. Even morning wood is a rarity.

"I'm Shaun Cleary, formerly of the Jameson pack, white witch and wolf, shaman to those who need it... *and deserve it...* No harm to me or mine and you are welcome to my home Alphas Heartstone and Jameson and King Edward. Break guesting laws and you will most definitely regret it."

64

I don't miss the fact that he specifically did NOT invite me in, and my wolf whimpers in response to the man's hostility. My beast wants Shaun to like us, but I can't figure out why...

There is a heaviness to the surrounding air for a few seconds before it suddenly lifts. With the freaky change in the atmosphere, the air smells more vibrant and I can sense the other people in the cabin. I hadn't realized until that moment that there was a veil between us.

MATE

My wolf howls in joy. This scent is indescribable. The closest thing I can bring to mind is chlorine and fruit punch, reminding me of summer days at the pool with Ric and Ethan and Alpha-Mate Annabelle when we weren't Alpha Heir and Beta Heir, but just boys having fun.

Before I can even approach my mate to pull him into the embrace my wolf is demanding, Shaun growls at me, stopping me in my tracks. The man looks at me like I'm dogshit stuck to his shoe before he storms off into the cabin.

Does he not know? I sift through my memories to try and figure out if there would be any reason Shaun wouldn't feel the mate bond...

"Connor, how about you stay with the cars, and I'll fill you in when we go to leave?" Ric pats me on the shoulder as he and Ethan's *other* relatives go into the cabin. I guess I wasn't needed here after all...

I have become obsolete.

Ethan has his father, grandfather, and mate to rescue him now. He doesn't need his big brother... no... *his cousin* anymore. My own mate doesn't even recognize me, so why should I be trusted to find my boy?

I hear a woman's raised voice from inside and I can't hold back the growl from my wolf. I just know she is yelling at my mate and my wolf refuses to allow that. No one gets to disrespect the mate of the Beta of the Jameson Pack...

Before I can fully contain my wolf, I feel rage explode out of Shaun. I don't waste any time breaking down the door and rushing to my mate. He is screaming under me and with each breath he takes it breaks my heart a little more. This is not only rage. This is terror. This is anguish. This is guilt...

"Shh... It's not your fault. It's all my fault. Blame me. Hate me..."

I keep it up like a mantra. He needs to let it go. He can blame me as much as he needs to. The gods know I blame myself enough. His hate can't make me hate myself more than I already do.

I didn't even notice the others leaving the room, but I focus only on calming my mate. I don't know how long it takes for Shaun to calm down, but the screams slowly turn to whimpers. I can only wrap myself around him tighter. My wolf is whining in my head, wanting to take away his pain. The only thing we can do is hold him, and I hate it. I'm a pathetic excuse for an alpha wolf...

"Let me go," he whispers despite nuzzling into my neck. "I don't want you to be my mate."

The shock of hearing those words is like falling through a frozen lake.

Mate doesn't want us. You did this! Mate hates you for not listening...

My wolf is berating me and I fucking deserve it...

I fall away from Shaun, staring at the shell of a man he has become in the last few minute. It's like he's aged a decade compared to the vibrant and beautiful man that I saw on the porch...

I did this. I destroy everyone who comes close...

Scrambling to my feet, I stagger out of the door, actively trying to not hear the gasping sobs from the man I'm leaving on the floor behind me. Every part of me wants to go back to him, to give him comfort in any way I can. Hell, he can beat on me, torture me, whatever he wants... I will do whatever he wants...

What he wants is for me to leave, so I step onto the porch. While my soul is shattering inside of me, I leave the last piece of my heart behind me on the floor.

"And that," says Edward, wiping his brow, "is why witches and werewolves should not mix."

"What is that supposed to mean?" I growl at the vampire. Rejected or not, no one gets to talk badly about my mate, even a fucking vampire king.

Ric reaches for me, but I smack his hand away. I don't deserve comfort, especially from him. His mate actually wants him even after all of the bullshit and pain he inflicted on our boy...

Edward acts like he is seeing nothing out of the ordinary and just answers the question...pretentious fucker. I almost want to piss him off so that he'll kill me now and end my misery. The only reason I'm even trying to restrain my wolf right now is the fact that I know that if Edward kills me, Ethan would be the one to suffer. He'd lose us both because the boy is loyal to a fucking fault.

"Witches get their power from emotions mostly. Werewolves need to be in control emotionally to keep the balance between their sides. When you combine the two, you get what you see..."

The vampire pointedly looks away from me to continue, "a young, uncontrolled child who could kill us all by accident if he gets too emotional. If raised under a kind and honorable Alpha, sometimes they survive and become stable. Outside of that? They are usually too dangerous to be allowed to live."

My growl is echoed by one from Ric and surprisingly Alpha Heartstone.

"That *boy* in there risked his own life for my son these days! He is under my protection," Bennet growls out to the apparent surprise of the vampire.

"Not that I should have to say it," Ric interjects, making sure that Edward is looking at him and not me, "But he's obviously the fated mate to my Beta, Ethan's brother, as well as being Ethan's best friend. Do you really think it's smart to threaten him when you just got your grandson back in your life?"

The realization that everyone is apparently aware of the fact that I just found my mate only makes the wound in my heart deeper. My wolf has fallen to whimpers in my head. I am barely hanging onto my humanity here.

"If Ethan didn't view me as a brother, would you even let me live?" I ask softly, looking directly at the vampire. "I'm the spawn of the evil things that destroyed him long before that lab got ahold of him. They loved me but did that to him! Don't I deserve to die, too?"

Falling to my knees, I try to think back to anything redeeming within me that I can use to help here and now. I need them to see the value in my mate, so that they can all work together...

I look to my best friend for help, but only see horror and pity in his eyes. Looking at the others in the area, that's all I see reflected back at me...

THEY KNOW.

The thought is overwhelming. My shame and disgrace is plain for everyone to see. I can't add to it. I can't show it. I am an alpha wolf. There is no weakness allowed...

Sweet boy, they don't deserve you...

Fuck! That voice again...

"Call me... when you're ready to get my brother back... or don't. I... I have to go. I can't wait here."

I don't even bother to undress before I shift. I can't give them a chance to talk to me right now. My wolf takes off into the trees, trying to outrun the cracks splintering my heart. Moments later, I let out a howl. I try to use it to release the pain and heartache I feel... But it doesn't work. I'm empty without my other half.

I was given a baby brother to protect, and I failed. I was given a mate, but I ignored his pleading for years. He saw how spectacular of a mess I really am and got out before I could bring him down as well. I deserve this...

They'll get Ethan back without me... then I can let go. I can finally let it all go. Now that I know I'm not abandoning anyone, I can go once Ethan is safe...

Connor Sinclair, you are an idiot...

Here comes a new voice. Too bad it doesn't know me at all...

16

SHAUN

It took less than twenty four hours for the situation with Ethan and the fae to be resolved, and all I can say is I'm glad it's over. Going without sleep for so long after my weekly shift ended was way too much for my overworked system. I never thought I would be thankful for a fae in my home, but Celeste came through with watching the kid while my body collapsed into sleep after the others left for Georgia.

Turns out Celeste is also a pediatric nurse, so I managed to hook her up with a position at the hospital with me. The gods know we could always use more assistance in keeping the unlawful fae away from kids. That's part of the reason I went into obstetrics. There will be ZERO changeling situations with me around...

It's not that all fae are kid-snatchers, but they operate by their own set of rules for the most part. I took the time to learn most of them, to protect myself and Zach during our time in Atlanta, but sometimes even they have people who go by the exact letter of the law, not the spirit of it. They are supposed to follow human laws in human lands, but there are always loopholes for those who go looking for them. That's why I am stoked to have the assistance at the hospital. Our area is on their radar now...

Alpha Heartstone put Celeste and her brother, Felix, up in an apartment near the university in his pack. Felix is apparently taking some courses. I don't know what he is taking them for, but it is long past time for him to stop living off of his sister. I don't have all of the details, but he seems like he needs someone else to tell him what to do. Even though, that's kind of my schtick, the boy is too needy for me.

It is now my last day off before my next two weeks of hell, so I am doing what I should have been doing for the last three days... cleaning. I put it off as long as I could, but even with my exhaustion, I couldn't keep leaving it like it was. Zach on the other hand? I don't think the man knows what cleaning is. Part of the reason I refuse to go to his house is the fact that I'm slightly terrified to see his living conditions without a roommate for three years.

My cleaning is interrupted by a text message notification on my phone... speak of the devil

> When r we gonna talk about this mate thing?
> 😅

> When u get ur ass to my cabin. Not doin the public thing except work 4 a while.

I somehow finally managed to get him to use actual emojis for a change and chuckle at the response I received. I didn't think he knew there was a middle finger one, but he put it in about six times before he said he was on his way over. Finishing up the counters in the kitchen, I put away the cleaning supplies and boot up my PS-5 while I wait.

After about an hour of carjacking and beating up pimps in GTA, my horribly repressed teacher friend is knocking on my door. As usual, he doesn't wait for an answer before coming right in. The scent wafting in the door behind him has me dropping the controller. Why the fuck is Connor's scent on my former roommate?!

Mate is MINE! my wolf growls and I have to make a concentrated effort to keep it inside of me.

Zach sets the fast food he's carrying down on my little table and giggles at the look on my face. Somehow, I didn't catch it in time and my wolf lets a growl escape. I shouldn't care if Connor is around Zach. It makes no difference to me. He is the one who ran from me...

You told him to go.

"I'm guessing that growl is because of the mate you refuse to speak of for the last month?" he asks as he pops a fry into his mouth. After chewing he tells me, "You should probably check your porch if you're wondering about the scent. I think his wolf wants to get on your good side."

I get up and go to the window to see what the hell my friend is talking about. My jaw drops and it takes me a minute to register what I'm seeing. To a normal human, having a dead animal carcass dropped on your porch would be a reason to call the cops. That is some serial killer behavior in humans. But with wolves? That's a love letter...

Mate wants us.

I tell my wolf to shut up even though I want to smile at the fact that he's got some of his energy back. Yeah, Connor's wolf wants his mate. His wolf never did anything wrong. It's the man that is the problem.

"Dumbass man doesn't even listen to his own wolf," I mutter to myself. Obviously, I forgot that my friend was happily munching on his nuggets and fries behind me, so the snort of laughter and resultant choking sounds come as a surprise.

"So you ever gonna admit that you want him?" Zach asks after downing half of his soda to wash down whatever he inhaled. I'm so glad I don't have to deal with his sugar rushes anymore. No one over the age of fifteen should get sugar rushes like this man does. "I mean, have you even had *anyone* yet?"

I can feel the blush heating my cheeks in response to his question. I know I don't have to answer. The color red that my face has become is answer enough. I mean, it's kind of wrong to lose your virginity when you are a literal child surrounded by college kids. Then, when I finally became an adult, I was so busy being an intern that I didn't have time for sex. Now that I'm in my residency, I'm still really busy, but I can't bring myself to go looking for it since I scented my mate...

"You know about what I like," I tell him. "It's bad enough I'm still a virgin at almost twenty one, but add into it that I wear the fancy lingerie and it's just asking for a misunderstanding. You know I'd likely end up with some dumbass thinking he gets to be all Super-Dom with me. Can you imagine? I don't have a submissive bone in my body!"

I watch Zach's face turns an unnatural shade of red as he struggles to hold in his laughter. He only releases it when I finally crack a small smile. He's been witness to a few times when a guy tried to get all toppy with me when he visited me up in Charleston after I turned eighteen. I might be trim, but my six foot height is enough to give me the leverage I need to throw someone around. I may be young, but I've spent my whole life being the little guy, the young guy. I hold my own quite well.

Just because I wear lacy underwear doesn't mean I am going to be the one on my knees or bending over... I would much rather see a certain alpha wolf on his knees, maybe with my dick in his...

That thought brings me back to reality and the smile falls away from my face...

"That right there is yet another reason why fate got it wrong," I sigh and let my head fall back against the wall. "Can you ever imagine an alpha wolf accepting a submissive role to a beta? It will never happen."

Zach gets up from the table and pulls me into a hug. This right here is the friend who held me through every nightmare during the years we were roommates. Now, he holds me through the tears that fall for the mate I can never have. I can't change who I am.

17

CONNOR

I can't get what I overheard out of my head. I didn't mean to follow Zach to the cabin, but outside of staking out the hospital, it was the only chance I've had this entire month of possibly catching a glimpse of Shaun. I know in my head that he doesn't want me, but my wolf won't let go... and right now I'm glad for that. Now, I know what the real hurdle is for us.

I thought the big issue was the fact that I ignored him for so long. It just hurt so much remembering Ethan during that time to the point that I ignored and threw away my mate's pleading for help. I was a selfish dumbass...

Told you to listen to him. Human never listens to wolf, my wolf grumbles at me for the millionth time since we scented our mate. *At least I'm trying to make it right.*

I chuckle at his method, remembering the look on Shaun's face today through the window. I was watching from the woods in my wolf form so that we wouldn't scare him off with our scent. When I saw the ghost of a smile, I cheated and used my hearing ability on Zach to listen in. I kind of feel guilty about it since he mumbled something about going to a clinic for a possible ear infection at the end, but I needed to know what my mate is thinking.

Hearing that Shaun enjoys wearing lacy underthings definitely made my dick wake up and take notice. It was like a lightning bolt hitting me to say to trust in fate... Shaun is most assuredly the perfect man for me.In high school, I always loved the look of the lingerie on models, so when the guys were passing around the magazines and lingerie catalogues, I was properly appreciative. They all assumed I was reacting to the women, but it was apparently the lace and satin itself that I enjoyed looking at.

The girls in the pack had all tried to seduce me at one time or another, the same way they did with Ric and Max. Max never hid that he was gay, so I'm not sure why they bothered. Ric was most definitely not, or at least he didn't show any preference towards guys, considering he slept his way through most of the girls in our high school. As the next Alpha, he told me there was no point in thinking about his sexuality because it was his duty to produce the next generation. Since there were no omegas anywhere near our pack, he'd have to take a woman as his mate.

I didn't have an issue with the girls. I just never felt anything more than appreciation for them unless they were wearing lingerie. Even then, as soon as the lacy things came off, my dick lost interest. It took until the disastrous college trip for me to realize what it was that I was actually attracted to. Once Ric dragged me into that frat party and I saw a man wearing a lace teddy across the room, I realized it was my holy grail of horny fuel. We were only supposed to be there for an hour, but Mr. Teddy caught me looking and one thing led to another. I lost my virginity to a random human guy on a naked mattress in a room that smelled of beer, vomit, and piss...

Remembering how awful I felt afterward makes me remember what else happened that night. While I was getting my ass railed, my parents were already dead and my little brother was sold to a lab by our uncle. That little tidbit helps me remember why I don't deserve to be happy. I don't deserve to have such perfection for a mate.

Climbing my back steps, I shift back from wolf to man and go inside my house. I don't even bother to clean off the mud and muck from the run home. I collapse on the couch to welcome the darkness.

It's the only thing I deserve after all. This loneliness and emptiness consuming me is only right. I fail everyone. I shouldn't set Shaun up to be hurt by me.

I just need to see Ethan give birth safely. Once that's done, I will leave before I can hurt anyone else.

18

CONNOR

> Can you come over tomorrow? I want to see my big brother on my birthday.

The text from Ethan pulls me from the fugue state I've been in since my wolf's latest attempt at courting our mate. It's like the more I give up, the harder he tries to win Shaun over. It's a losing battle. The man deserves so much more that I can give him. So does my brother. I need to get him prepared for life without me, so I send him a message back.

> Sorry, buddy. I have to miss your birthday, but I'll come visit soon.

I barely have the chance to drop the phone back to the floor when I'm hit with a blast of pain so intense that I break the coffee table with my grip. What in the fuck was that?!

You hurt him. You hurt boy. Grow up and protect.

It takes a second to be able to breathe through this anguish to make sense of what my wolf is growling to me. I hurt Ethan? I mean, yeah, his birthday is tomorrow but we've never celebrated...

Damnit! We've never celebrated his birthday...

My mother used it as an excuse for networking. He got a picture next to the cake and then the adults stood around. I never really noticed because Ric and I would run off to play. I had always assumed that he did as well... This is yet another instance of me being the world's worst big brother ever. Why the fuck does Ethan even care if I'm there? I've never done a damn thing for him. He should hate me...

I hate me...

I'm hating you, too my wolf grumbles at me before going back to ignoring me.

After a while, I feel my Alpha outside of my house. He couldn't just let me be. I know I fucked up with Ethan, but what am I supposed to do about it now?

Glancing out the window, I see he's standing at the end of my drive on the phone. I cheat a bit and use my ability to listen in.

"Ric? It's Shaun. Is Ethan alright?"

My curiosity is going to be the death of me. The sound of my mate's voice brings a measure of peace that I don't deserve, but I can't resist holding the connection to listen in.

"He's getting there, but your wall is gone," Ric tells him, turning back to the house. I step away from the window before he can notice me watching. "He got a text and it sent him into the mother of all panic attacks."

"Ok good," Shaun exhales before stammering, "I mean, not good as in he had a panic attack, but good that it was just the wall crashing under force. I felt it break and was worried with what tomorrow is and... and... and he's been so stressed and trying to hide it and..."

"Breathe, Shaun," Ric says. "What's this about tomorrow? It's just his birthday."

The pause on the other end of the line makes me wonder if maybe they noticed me listening in. I take the chance to look out again only to see Ric looking confused staring at the tree line behind the house.

"Um Alpha..."

Shaun stops and starts a few times before finally coming out and saying what is bothering him. "Ethan's birthday is also the anniversary of both his mother's and grandmother's death. Both died in childbirth. And he's pregnant... Early labor is not only possible, but expected for both omegas and multiples..."

The shock of what my mate has just revealed throws off my concentration and I slide down the wall next to the window. It takes me a few seconds to realize I need to re-establish my link to listen in to their conversation. I don't know if I missed anything, but I don't think so.

"He asked me yesterday if the babies would be able to live if something happened to him at this point in the pregnancy. I didn't put it together until just now with the wall crashing," Shaun says, basically ripping my heart out. "Ric, I truly believe he thinks he's going to die tomorrow like his mother and grandmother. I just didn't realize it until I thought something actually happened with the wall coming down."

"He's not dying tomorrow. He's not dying in childbirth. My boy is going to be around to raise these kids with all the love and support that he never got for himself," Ric growls into the phone.

There's a lull in their conversation, but I can feel my wolf agreeing with his Alpha's sentiments. There's no way we will let anything happen to Ethan...

"What set him off? Who sent the text?" Shaun asks, breaking the silence, and I know it's time for me to get my ass up and answer the door before my Alpha breaks it down. I break the connection and go face the music. It's no less than what I deserve.

I open the door to see Ric with his fist raised to knock. The is the first time he's seeing me in over a month and from his face, I can tell I look rough. Come to think of it, when was the last time I took a look in a mirror?

"Whatever the fuck your problem is with your mate, fix it!" he snarls pushing past me into the house. "You are GOING to see your brother tomorrow and you are GOING to be happy and not look like a homeless drug addict. Consider it an order from your Alpha."

I flop down on the couch, waiting for whatever else Ric is going to throw at me today. It is blatantly obvious he's not done with me yet. I want to refuse his order, but in the end, there's no point. I *must* make things right with Ethan. I didn't realize he was already worrying about so much.

"What the fuck happened to you, dude?" he sighs as he moves some trash to lean against the arm of a chair.

I throw my forearm over my eyes to block the little bit of moonlight filtering into the room through the curtains. This isn't about me.

"Is Ethan alright? I know I hurt him, but I honestly didn't think it would hit him like that." I try to choke back the sobs that are threatening to escape..."I can't stop hurting him, can I?"

Ric's silence speaks volumes. Did I even ask that out loud or was it just in my head? I don't even know anymore. Keeping up the façade that I am fine is getting more and more difficult. The babies need to come soon. I don't know how much longer I can keep the mask in place.

"If I promise to be there tomorrow, just for a bit, will you let it go for now?" I ask, hoping it will be enough to get him out of my house. I'm going to fall apart again, and I refuse to do so in front of my best friend. It hurts so much to keep up the appearance that I can function as a human being, but no one can see me crack... Betas don't fold under pressure...

Ric sighs and gives me a nod before turning to leave. As soon as he's outside, I turn the deadbolt on the door. I can't handle any more visitors today... especially if I'm going to have to deal with the people at the party tomorrow. I need to rebuild the mask that everything is fine. I'm not going to ruin Ethan's party...

19

SHAUN

Standing in the kitchen waiting for the birthday boy to wake up is kind of tense for me. I don't want to be here, in this house. This is the pack that drove me away when I was a child. This room is full of the Alphas and leaders who belittled me and turned away from me...

Stop it, Shaun. You're an adult now and they all know the error of their ways back then. Talking to myself as a separate entity.. yeah, I'm doing just fine in the fucking Jameson pack. But I remind myself that Ethan is safe and here and...

And apparently he's stuck at the top of the steps because he woke up half regressed...

Getting to know his little side over the last few months has been interesting. As kids, he was never all that into playing or anything that would involve attention, but now? Little Ethan is freaking great. He's uninhibited and giggles and loves wholeheartedly. He's like a little brother to me, and I have been so happy to see him finally get to be the child he was meant to be back then.

When I first got here, Ric told me that he's broadcasting his thoughts again, but I didn't think it was this bad. Maybe he'll get more of a handle on it as he wakes up more?

No such luck. Every single fear and morose thought flows

through all of our heads while on the outside the boy looks like he just won the lottery. How the hell is he doing it? I never knew just how doom and gloom my BFF was inside his head. I knew shit was bad for him as a kid, but he *always* had a smile. I never knew exactly how bad it was growing up in that house until getting to see his memories at the cabin. How in the fuck this guy still laughs and smiles is beyond me...

"Shaun, is there anything you can do to put the wall back up?" Ric asks, breaking into my inner monologue.

Am I broadcasting again? Ethan asks through his mind speak and everyone in the room is nodding emphatically. I can't stop the chuckle that escapes me. He is so freaking adorable when he starts regressing.

"Shaun?" Ric asks again with a laugh.

"Almost done," I say from the other end of the room. It takes a lot more concentration to do it without touching Ethan, but I wanted to give his family a chance to give him all the comfort and hugs and touching. That's not me. I'm just the friend.

I finally relax when I feel the wall click in place. It's a bit flimsy compared to the last one, but I'll reinforce it as the day goes on. This was just a quick and dirty patch job.

"When did it go down?" my bestie asks me when I join him at the island where Ric put him up on a stool.

"Last night, little one," Ric says. "When you were screaming, the wall shattered."

Ethan looks like he's committed the worst possible atrocity, hanging his head in shame... "Sorry..."

"You don't have to apologize for someone else's behavior!" I growl. My eyes seek out the reason in question, the person who was callous enough to hurt his brother... his high risk pregnant omega brother.

The only thing that hurts worse than knowing that this man is the one fate seems to think is a good match for me, is the fact that the birthday boy still looks at him like he hung the moon... and that I know if he touched me, I would fold like a bad hand in poker.

Felix has good timing, coming up to give Ethan a hug and explain that he has to leave. From the rushed conversation, I gather that I am not the only one that fate has decided to fuck over in the mate department. When the fae boy leaves, I decide to follow. I have a quick word with Celeste and make my own escape. I'll let Ethan keep his hero worship, but I refuse to watch it.

20

SHAUN

"I can't believe I let you talk me into this!"

The volume of Ethan's shout isn't exactly an indicator to his frustration with me. The Impala doesn't have AC and early August in South Carolina means the windows are down, even at six in the morning. I finally got the driver's side window un-stuck to go down, but now the rear passenger side window won't go all the way back up... Plus, I think I might need a new muffler...

As his obstetrician, I've been struggling these last few months since the birthday party to convince Ethan to come in for an ultrasound. There's only so much my magic can sense with his pregnancy, and I'd feel a million times better getting my best friend in for a real exam with real equipment.

I mean, I get it. His fear of doctors is one hundred percent reasonable for him, but in good conscience, I can no longer let him put himself and the babies at risk. There is no getting out of this appointment. If he bails on this, we are going to have to resort to some less than ethical and legal measures to ensure the babies are good.

Pulling into my parking space, I get out of the car and walk around to Ethan's side. He is really struggling with this and the whine coming from his throat has me worried that he's going to...

I have to catch myself against the side of the car. Yep. There goes the wall again.

Three months of building and fortifying the wall in his head to keep his abilities under control and pulling into a parking space just shattered it all.

Fuck! It's going to be a long ass day for my day off.

Nope. I can't do this. I can't go inside. Last time I was here, the fae wanted to kidnap me. The time before that, a doctor scared the shit out of me and didn't even care. Before that was when I first came out of the lab and was still in survival mode.

Well... actually I suppose I was here when I was dead after that gathering thingy, but I wasn't alive for that so I don't count it...

What is that weird high pitched whining noise coming from the car? Maybe Shaun should get a professional to look at it. If he ever gets his head out of his ass with Connie, he'd look at it. My big brother has always been great with cars and bikes and really anything with moving parts...

I knock on the window to cut off Ethan's thoughts that are spilling out. I don't need any more reminders of Connor and what he can do for me. I haven't seen him since the birthday party, although I am happy to know he is at least making appearances with his brother to the extent where Ethan isn't worried about him. It's like he's waiting for my shifts at the hospital to come by the house in order to avoid me, and part of me hates that.

I need Daddy for this... Ethan's thoughts are clear on his face even though he's still broadcasting them.

"Your Daddy is already here," I say through the window. "He just parked his SUV and is walking over. Now, unlock the door so that I can yank you upright and fix your wall again."

"You alright, baby?" Ric asks, clearing the back end of the Impala while I do my best to resist helping the pregnant man get up from the seat. He lets out a growl to show his frustration with being brought to the hospital, but I don't give a fuck at this point. I'm a doctor, a freaking baby doctor at that. My patients' health is all that matters to me in this situation.

I chuckle at the way my omega bestie melts into his Daddy's arms. Closing the door on my own baby, I manage a small bit of hope for something I might actually be able to accomplish. One day soon, she'll be as cherry as Dean's Baby...

Clearing my throat, I lead my charges to the main hospital entrance opposite the emergency room. Just turning in that direction helps to calm Ethan a little bit. I don't remember him being brought into the E.R. but based on his explosion of thoughts a few minutes ago, he must have been brought in when I was not on shift...

"It looks like Godzilla ate a baby shower and then threw up in the lobby!" Ethan exclaims as soon as we step off the elevator and proceeds to slam his hand over his mouth. His eyes are wide in surprise.

No one bothers to hold back their amusement at the statement. Hell, I've made similar remarks a few times myself, but the administration seems to think that our floor needs to look like the inside of a Pepto Bismol bottle.

The nurses take the happy couple to one of the exam rooms while I head to storage to get the machines we need. Ethan's nerves are coming back, so I'm going to be limiting the exposure for him to myself, Savannah, and one other nurse. My usual choice for the second nurse would have been the witch who works in oncology, but she has a sick mother or something. Nancy is alright, but she's human.

When I come back to the room, I manage to convince Ethan, with Ric's help, to climb onto the bed and get his feet in the stirrups so that I can take a look. I have to put on my "doctor hat" to do this... Never in a million years did I ever think I would be spending an early morning looking at my best friend's asshole and feeling around it. Those types of feelings were never in the picture for us...

"Looks good down here, Buddy," I tell him, sitting back up. "Let's get some pictures and we can get you out of here before the place starts to fill up for the morning."

I roll the stool across the floor so that I can bring the ultrasound machine over next to the bed. I trust the nurses to be able to get him ready while I untangle the cord stuck in the wheel. Why can't people make sure the cords are tucked away properly?

"Ready to get the first photos of the future models?" Nancy asks as she lifts up Ethan's shirt to uncover his belly. He jumps at the contact and my decision to do this before the official opening of the hospital is cemented as the right choice. I don't need him freaking out and letting out another psychic blast.

Even after warming it, the gel for the ultrasound feels weird for some people. When I squirt some on Ethan's belly, it is apparently cold enough that he lets out a string of cussing that makes the human nurse blush and Savannah snort. Apparently, that snort draws Ethan's attention to her.

"How do I know you?" he asks her, causing her to chuckle.

"Remember your Christmas shopping accident?" she responds with a smirk.

There's an element of joy to my bestie's face when he makes the connection. I vaguely remember something... Oh... OH! The incident with Doctor Douche was with ETHAN!?!

I hate the reminder that I should have had my best friend back over a year ago... He was *here*! The fact that my best friend was alive and well and close by, but not a single soul bothered to let me know weighs heavy in my gut. They *knew* I was still looking for him. They fucking *knew* I was close by. They had my return address. They had my email...

I feel my magic starting to flicker in response to my anger. Can't let it out... I have to focus on Ethan and the babies...

"Daddy, can we invite her to the next cookout?" Ethan asks Ric while I reposition the wand to get a clearer picture of what I think I'm seeing...Focus... "She sent the meanie doc flying last time. I like her!"

Ric just chuckles and tells Savannah she's more than welcome to visit them whenever she wants, to which she gives a full belly laugh and agrees to come, especially after the babies are here. Holy shit... they are *definitely* going to need the help.

Holy cock-sucking twat-waffles... This never fucking happens in supes. Hell, it rarely happens in humans.

"E-man... Ric... I don't know how to tell you this," I start to say, but I guess I didn't school my tone enough since my bestie does what he does best lately and jumps straight to panic. Before I can say anything else, Ric is trying to calm him down.

"Easy there, Blue. Let him finish," Ric chides gently. Ethan takes a few deep breaths to try and relax, then nods for me to continue. I make sure he's good before I continue, trying to make my voice sound more like his friend than his doctor.

"Early on, both my magic and Celeste's recognized you were having twins," I tell them, giving them both serious eye contact. It's the complete and honest truth. Three months ago, it was most definitely twins... now?

Ric and Ethan both nod, but then the wall I repaired less than an hour ago in the parking lot shatters like a greenhouse hit by a locomotive.

21

SHAUN

DID I LOSE ONE OF THE BABIES?!?! Did the bitch take one after all????

Everyone in the room grabs their head while I struggle to regain enough control to block Ethan's outburst from reigning chaos on the entire hospital.

I don't know what's wrong with them, but I'm gonna be going to fuck up a Goddess in a minute here as soon as I can make sure I'm not going to put my remaining baby in danger...

"Shit, man! Chill!" I scream at the omega. "Quit blasting my walls to fucking splinters!"

It takes a minute or two to recreate enough of a barrier in his head to stop the leaking. I can't keep doing this from the outside. I'm going to have to be around him twenty four seven now. There's no way to do a remote patch if this is what his psychic blasts are going to be like for the next couple months until the babies get here.

"OK, so OW!" Savannah says as she starts distributing some ibuprofen and bottles of water. My other nurse is passed out but otherwise fine. Nancy is so getting herself whatever the fuck she wants for this... my treat. This is why we usually don't let humans treat the supes unless it's an emergency. They're too fragile.

"Ow is right," I reply as I massage my left temple. "As I was saying before you overreacted and jumped to the absolute *worst* possible conclusion...

"Back in March, both me and Celeste only sensed two babies. Felix could only sense there was more than one. The reason I wanted to do the ultrasound so badly is the fact that although yes, you're almost seven months along, you are WAY bigger than you should be with just twins."

Ethan looks completely lost, but Ric manages to catch on pretty quickly. I see the joy mingling with trepidation on his face.

"How many babies are we talking about here, Shaun?" he asks and we all watch the change in Ethan when it finally registers to *him* what we're saying. I struggle to hold back the laughter his expression is bringing out in me. It looks like he is trying to smile while choking on something, his mouth opening and closing like a goldfish during feeding time...

"Just three," I barely manage to get out without laughing. "But it means I'm basically moving in with you guys until they come out. You wanna know what you're having?"

The two of them look at each other and my bestie nods his head like a bobblehead that someone just tapped. This right here is what I always want to see in my patients. It's even more special when my best friend is the one filled with joy.

"Two boys and a girl," says Savannah as she tucks a blanket around the other nurse. "The boys are likely identical if you had two turn into three."

I nod my agreement while I start putting the ultrasound cart back in order... the CORRECT way this time. The happy couple is being all lovey dovey right now, and if anyone deserves it, it would be Ethan. I can't really find the energy in me to hide my envy, so I help Savannah to get Nancy up and head back to the lobby. I figure it's the least I can do to let the happy parents to be celebrate without me mucking it up with my own emotions.

As we reach the lobby, the absolute last person that should ever be on this floor is just getting off the elevator. I turn my back to him to help my nurse into the chair in the office, making sure she's not suffering any ill effects. The douchebag can wait as far as I'm concerned, but Savannah goes right on the attack.

"Doctor Delphi," Savannah states firmly, backing the asshole up away from the hallway to the exam rooms. "You have no business on this floor and there are no patients for you to see."

I don't have to be looking to know he's sneering his signature trust fund never had to work a day in my life smirk when he shoots back at her, "You're nothing but a damn nurse, Savannah! You're lucky I didn't take your job back in December for that stunt you pulled!"

I have absolutely had it with this pompous, self-righteous asshat of a douchenozzle claiming to be a fucking doctor... Today is not the day to fuck with me. Not now. Not when I'm feeling like absolute shit for wanting a man who doesn't want me back who I won't be able to avoid for the foreseeable future...

"Doctor Delphi! You have no business on this floor and you sure as hell have no authority to talk to MY nurse in that way!" I state forcefully as I approach from behind Savannah. "Get the FUCK out of my department before I tell Edward that you keep ignoring the rules of this hospital that he himself set forth."

I purposely bring up his king to try and end this without losing my cool. Growling barely audibly, I add, "Or would you rather me tell your king that *you're* the one who is upsetting his grandson?"

Doctor Douche still has the nerve to try and push past me, but both my wolf and my magic come to the front to push him back. The elevator doors open without anyone pushing a button and I shove the piece of shit into the car. I'm half disappointed that it isn't the empty shaft. If anyone deserves to be thrown down an elevator shaft, it's this twat.

My magic has never liked him and I can't figure out exactly why. I mean, he's a fucking asshole, but that's not a reason for my magic to dislike him. If it was, half the damn hospital would be getting my hackles raised... actually more like half the county... But this guy? He claims to be half vampire, but that smells false to me. At the same time, he scents as human plus a little something else. He's a mystery and a c-word, so I distrust him. After his behavior today, I'm wondering how the fuck the board approved his return from suspension...

Savannah and I head back to the exam room after making sure Nancy knows to alert us immediately if *anyone* gets off the elevator. I expect to see my bestie and his mate still being all lovey with each other, but Ethan looks terrified. The closest I've ever seen to this look on his face is when he had to go home with blood on his clothing as a kid, and that was nothing compared to this. This is something primal.

"Is the voice gone?" Ethan whispers, hugging himself as tight as possible. "He can't know I'm pregnant. He'll want me back. He can't know. I can't go back. I won't go back! He can't have me! He can't have them!"

Ethan is getting hysterical and I know I am not going to be able to hold back the next psychic blast with this level of panic...

I can only brace myself and hope that my mind and magic are strong enough to save the lives of the people in this hospital...

Luckily, Ric sees the situation for what it is and acts quickly. He uses his power as Alpha to send Ethan to sleep. I usually despise Alpha's using their control over their pack members like this, but it's a good thing in this situation. The stress isn't good for the babies, nor for papa... not to mention the fallout of what his hysteria could cause...

Staring at the other two wolves in the room, I wonder... just how long am I going to have to be the one to do what the fuck is necessary for this man? When the fuck will these alphas get their shit together and stop failing the rest of us?

22

CONNOR

It's been two weeks since my little brother's psychic blast rocked the hospital, and I've been trying to track that evil fucker ever since. Ric explained everything that happened to me that day they learned they were having triplets, and it's been my mission since then to find and destroy one Doctor Delphi.

Turns out, the guy isn't even a real doctor, let alone any relation to any vampire. Edward is pissed that there was an imposter claiming to be part of his kingdom, but one would think he'd be more upset at the fact that Ethan revealed this monster is the one behind the lab where he was held for eight years.

Destroy him, my wolf growls. I wholeheartedly agree. We will absolutely destroy this monster.

Using my sight ability, I've managed to figure out that Delphi hasn't left the area, but I can't get close to him. By the time I get to the place I see through his eyes, he's gone. It's almost like he's getting some kind of divine intervention. Nothing in any research I've done over the last few months shows that clairvoyance is real outside of a particular family of witches... but I already checked them out and they are so very insular that they don't even allow their members to leave, let alone coordinate with other races.

I'm using my ability again while I take a rushed shower to see where the douche might be when the message alert goes off on my phone. Switching back to my own eyes, I grab my phone, thankful for the waterproofing of modern technology, and open the group message that Jackie started.

BABIES ARE COMING

I don't need to see any more than that. I hurriedly use voice to text while rinsing the shampoo out of my hair. I don't even know what is being sent until I get my shoes on and take a look. I have to laugh at the way the artificial intelligence interpreted my garbled words through the water...

Finishing shoulder ant bee sum too mountains mast i gut kit you go good lust

Chuckling I throw on the first pair of pants and t-shirt I grab from my drawers and race for my truck. Speeding off to the Alpha's house, I know I'll be there in under a minute. Another few texts hit before I pull up to the house.

Before I can even read them, I have Max and Ric jumping in the truck, telling me to haul ass to the hospital. I don't question it but put the pedal to the floor. They explain that Edward and his nephew Josh used their vampire speed to get Ethan and Shaun there faster. Makes sense to me.

We're about halfway there when my phone rings. Thankful for the Bluetooth connection in the truck, I answer. It's Zach Morrison, the elementary teacher. Why is he calling me?

"Um... Beta Connor, do you have the Alpha with you?" he asks when I answer.

Ric glances at the console before answering, "I'm here Zach. Is everything alright with Jackie?"

Okay that makes sense. I kind of forgot that someone would need to be there with the kid while we all raced off to the hospital. That was supposed to be me, but I guess Mr. Morrison was there already.

"Jack is fine," the teacher says with an exaggerated sigh. "He also pointed out that you guys forgot the go-bag for Ethan that was in the back of the SUV. I have it here in my hand if you want me to bring it?"

Part of me is holding back the laughter at the situation. Here we are, three alpha wolves, being put in our place by the tiny wisp of a beta elementary school teacher. Oh, the irony.

"Is Mr. Whiskers in the bag?" Max asks before Ric can respond.

I slam on the brakes. I'm lucky we're not on a busy road. There is not a chance in the nine levels of hell that Ethan will forgive us if Mr. Whiskers isn't there to greet the babies.

I don't wait for the others to respond before I'm pulling a U-turn and racing back to the house. I am going to be the one to give him that teddy. I gave him Mr. Whiskers in the first place to protect him from his nightmares. No nightmares today...

"We're coming back for the bag," I say as I push the truck even harder to get back to the house. "Meet us at the driveway."

Hanging up the call, I hope and pray that we don't miss the births for this detour. But I *know* Ethan would want Mr. Whiskers there more than anything else in the world...more than his big brother at least.

23

SHAUN

Vamp speed is kind of cool, but definitely not my preferred way to travel. Once we get to the hospital, I'm able to put some wards up on the room we put Ethan in so that his contractions aren't debilitating everyone in a ten mile radius.

Holy fuck, those hurt. Makes me glad I'm a beta wolf. Joys of childbirth? No thank you.

"MOTHER-FUCKING-SHIT-FUCK-DAMN-FUCKING-SHIT-BALLS-DONKEY-TITS!"

Savannah and I both chuckle at the string of creative profanities that keep coming out of Ethan's mouth. His big bad vampire king grandfather literally fled the room once we were safely here, but his cousin Josh stuck behind. I thought I saw him at the birthday party but wasn't sure. He's been a big help here so far, and his humor is right on track with my own.

Again, there's something more niggling at the back of my mind. It takes a while, but I finally remember him. He's not the same goth teenager that ran off after listening to my sob story when I was thirteen. He ditched the guyliner and black clothing for the worn jeans and graphic tee look. He also looks like a wet dream for me, but neither is now the time nor am I interested... Wish I was though...

As the latest contraction subsides, Josh glances at me and I can see the instant he recognizes me back. I can't believe the fates brought us together again like this. Why couldn't they have sent him back into my life before I came back here, before I scented my mate?

You're the one who sent me to look for him all those years ago, right? He sends to my head. I smile and nod to him.

I'm sorry I couldn't free him...

The sorrow and guilt radiating off of this young vampire is heart-breaking, but the sounds from the monitors tell me I have to check on my patients...

"Okay, E-man," I say, wiping the sweat from his forehead. "It shouldn't be much longer. You're almost there, but I'm guessing we have about an hour."

The look on my best friend's face at the thought of going through this for another hour is hilarious, but I somehow manage to keep the smile hidden. Josh isn't as successful and gets a kick to the groin for his trouble... There is a reason I made sure I was by his head before I said anything.

"We are going to go out and update everyone," I tell him once I can control my laughter at the vampire's pain. "Do you want your Daddy in here or have him wait for the big finale?"

Ethan looks up at me with pleading in his eyes. "I don't want him to see me in pain. It makes him sad. I want him to be happy in this room."

I nod and grip his hand tightly before Savannah and I leave the room. We head to the waiting area to update his family. Like an invisible tether is between us, my eyes immediately seek out Connor. He is beside *his* best friend, holding his hands tightly. They both look horribly tense.

Savannah starts updating everyone while I'm struggling to fix whatever is suddenly making my magic go haywire with the wards around the room. Either the contractions are getting stronger or...

"The room is silent," Edward says and zips past me toward the room where his nephew and grandson are.

Shit! Something is very fucking wrong. I can't sense anything in the room...

I race after him, along with every alpha wolf present, only to find the door is locked and we can't break it down. Something has usurped my magic and trapped us all outside of the room. Then, like a nightmare come to life, the door disappears.

No! I can't lose him again! He's not gone! He's NOT gone!

I feel my knees give out, but all of my focus is on keeping my hold on the magic inside of me. I can't let it go. Not here... I would kill us all...

Before my body can hit the floor, I feel strong arms wrapped around me, holding me up. It takes a few moments for me to hear the words he's whispering in my ear, only for me.

"He's not gone. We will get to him. We will save him. I got you. You're mine and I'm yours. I'm your tool. Use me."

"They aren't gone," Edward says snapping me back to full awareness. "I am hearing some of what Joshua is sending out. They believe him to be dead, so they left him be."

Ok. It's time to think rationally. I stand up on my own, but don't push Connor away just yet. It's selfish, but I'm pretty sure his touch is the only thing keeping me in control right now. If they are still there and Josh is able to communicate, that means it's just an illusion ward on the door. I can fix this if only I knew who subverted my own wards. It would take a level of power only the royal line of the fae or the gods possess...

"It's the perpetrator of the lab... and your Goddess who are behind this trickery," Edward sighs as he leans against the wall opposite where the door should be. "This fake is not only a sociopath, but apparently also a demigod. That's all I'm able to get. The bitch has pulled Ethan into her memories. Joshua cannot get through the wall in the boy's mind to see what he's seeing right now."

Shit. I made the wall too strong.

Before I can continue to beat myself up, Connor whispers in my ear.

"Not your fault, sweetheart."

I hate to say it, but the endearment from him makes me shiver in all the right places. Before my body has the opportunity to betray me, the door is suddenly back. Ric throws it open and ice flows in veins when I hear Josh screaming my name.

I push Connor away from me to rush into the room only to have one of my worst fears materialized.

My best friend is dead...

"Why won't he heal!?" Josh is screaming, trying to do CPR. "Ethan, you can't leave me again! I have to keep you safe!"

That sound of the fetal heartbeat monitor alarm finally registers and I push Josh to the floor. Savannah and Celeste come in and start pushing the rest of the family out of the room. I don't have time to pay attention to anyone else. I have to get the babies out. They are all I have left of him now. I can't fail them like I failed him.

This is *my* domain. The hospital is *my* territory. He should have been safe here...

"Get the C-Section tray! We're getting these babies out now!" I bellow. I trust Celeste and Savannah to get everything we need.

Josh is still on the ground muttering and crying. Every time someone tries to help him up or get him out of our way, he starts to go into hysterics. I don't have time for this shit.As Celeste trips over him for the third time, she looks at him and freezes. I know he's in shock, but I can't afford to have one of my nurses go into shock with him.

"Get him out of here!" I yell out over the sounds of Josh's ramblings, sobs, and screams. "If these babies are going to come out safely, I need to be able to move where he is!"

Max rushes forward and manages to scoop him into his arms. The boy clings to him for dear life and allows him to take him from the room when no one else could even come near. I don't have the time to think on that.

"He has to heal. He can't die. He's not *supposed* to die. It's all my fault. I couldn't save him...."

The sound of Josh's anguished ramblings is a distraction I don't need as I cut into my best friend's corpse to save his babies. I feel it when Connor leaves the room. His pain is so intense, it's a miracle he is even able to stand, let alone drag his Alpha from the room.

"Baby one is out," I mutter as I hand the baby over to Celeste and Savannah to get the cord clipped and the baby cleaned up.

"It's a boy," Celeste whispers. "And a beautiful little one at that, just like your papa."

I choke back the sob threatening to come out as I grab the next baby. Another boy. This time Savannah is the one gushing over him.

I can't stop the tears from falling as I lift out Ethan's baby girl and hear her piercing cry, which kicks off her brothers.

"Go ahead and cry kids," I whisper to her as I clean her off. "Your papa wouldn't want you to ever hold back."

Leaving her in the basket for someone else to take up to the nursery, I turn back to the body of my best friend. He looks... gruesome. I can do something about that, at least a little bit.

I'm not sure how long I spend stitching up and cleaning up the blood on the body, but it's finally done. Now that the body is whole, I can use my magic to fix the rest. Repairing a dead body doesn't require the same effort that healing a live on requires. I try to remove the bruising around his throat and the bloodshot eyes, but it doesn't work.

What the fuck? This is usually easy...

I have healed corpses before even when I can't use my magic to heal a living person. I should be able to do this. Okay, so those are injuries that were inflicted by a demigod. Maybe that's why I can't do anything about them? I've never tried to correct a god's misdeeds, so I don't really know.

Instead of beating a dead horse...

I chuckle before I can stop it. Ethan loved a poorly placed pun. The tears start flowing again. Maybe they never stopped in the first place...

I shift my focus to the cesarian incision to heal that. If it is a demigod thing, then I should be able to fix this up without a problem.

"FUCK!"

I fall to my knees next to the body, not caring that his cold and congealed blood is soaking through the knees of my jeans. Who cares at this point? I'm covered in the blood of the only person who ever showed me love and I couldn't save him. I barely managed to save his babies and they'll never know how utterly amazing their papa was...

It hardly registers when Connor picks me up from the floor. When it's obvious that my legs won't hold me, he sweeps me up into a bridal carry and walks us out of the room.

"Have faith, my beautiful witch," he whispers to me, setting me down on a bed in an empty room. "Ethan has magic in his blood from his father. We have to have faith."

My mate kisses my forehead and turns to leave. I'm pretty sure he believes me to be asleep when he utters, "I have to believe he'll come back. There's nothing else to live for if he's gone."

At that moment, I knew that losing my best friend wasn't the end of my world. This moment is. I just discovered I'm not enough for my mate to want to stay. I wasn't enough for my parents to love and apparently neither am I enough for a mate gifted to me by fate. And the only person who ever cared is gone.

24

SHAUN

It has been two weeks since that horrible night at the hospital, and I'm grabbing some much-needed caffeine from the kitchen in the Alpha house of the Jameson Pack. The least I can do is to help with the babies while we all wait for Ethan to come back to us. I'm still not fully convinced that he *will* come back, but everyone here has assured me that immortality is part of his heritage as a result of some curse or blessing or whatever from his father's bloodline.

There is not enough coffee in the world to wrap my brain around that while dealing with three screaming newborns. Babies who haven't had any type of paternal interaction from the time they came into the world. Ric is refusing to even look at them.

Fate, you really fucked it all up in the mate department, didn't you? I send my message into the ether, not expecting an answer, but manage to spill hot coffee down the front of my shirt when I get one.

He's awake now, a woman's voice whispers on a puff of wind.

I throw the half empty cup toward the sink, hearing it shatter but not giving a single fuck, as I race up the stairs to the room that Ethan shares with his mate. Panting in the doorway, I can't believe my eyes. He's really fucking here!

"Why do I hurt so much?" Ethan asks, looking down at his body in the bed.

I can't help it. When you leave the door wide open, I have to take advantage. "You've been mostly dead all day," I gasp out between breaths and watch his face light up upon seeing me. There's nothing but overwhelming joy in my heart right now.

"Can we watch Princess Bride tonight?" little Jack calls out from somewhere in the house and we all hear Max yelling back, "Again?!"

As Ethan tries to sit up, I rush forward and pull him gently into a hug. I can't stop my body from shaking, but the relief I feel can't be contained.

"Nothing would heal on your body," I breathe out. I'm sure he can hear the echo of the pain we all felt in my voice. "Then, about three days ago, the incision showed progress and then stopped healing. Yesterday, the bruising around your throat started to fade and then stopped... It made no sense. I was afraid you'd heal just to go away again..."

I hear him sigh and feel him push me away. I let him go when I see him reaching for his mate, but instead of helping Ethan, Ric backs away and tells him, "You need to rest and restore your strength. Everything else can wait."

I see the stubbornness in my best friend's face as he turns to me and holds up his arm for me to help him up. Glancing at Ric, I see something else behind his eyes. Nothing but pure unadulterated malice is pouring out of him. There's something else there... Ethan looks from my face to his mate and proceeds to flip the fuck out on him.

"What the fuck is going on here?" he snarls, pushing me aside to get up from the bed. "I come back from the dead and all of a sudden I don't get to make my own choices?"

He struggles to get his feet under himself, but the rage inside the Alpha is preventing me from reaching out to help him.

"If I want to get up from the fucking bed to go take a piss, I can do that, right?!"

Ethan is actually yelling at this point, and I'm surprised it hasn't brought anyone running. The feeling I'm getting from Ric is just so WRONG that I am afraid a tiny spark will set him off and be ruinous to us all...

Ric starts to reach for Ethan, but he pulls his hand back when Ethan lets out a growl. The Alpha doesn't even show that he's affected before he turns and leaves the room. Ethan just heads into the bathroom. With Ric out of the room, I can finally breathe.

While Ethan is busy with his bladder, Max and Jack come to the door with the babies, smiling ear to ear. I shake off the feeling from Ric and focus on the happy occasion of Papa Ethan meeting his little ones. I'll have to address the issue with the Alpha later because that was definitely something witchy and I need him safely away from innocents to take care of it.

I take one of the babies from Max's arms and wait for Ethan to be done in the bathroom. We've just got one parent back, now the other one is on the fritz...

As the proud papa is finally greeting his precious babies, Zander, Alec, and Tessa, I take a second to send up a thanks to the universe for Ethan coming back to us. At least now, I can stop worrying that my mate is going to leave them behind in addition to me...

Who am I kidding? I'm being selfish. Even if he doesn't want me, I can't live in a world where he doesn't exist. Fate was right on that point. I fucking love Connor Sinclair and always have. It shouldn't have taken losing Ethan for real for me to realize that.

Cuddling the infant in my arms, I can only hope that the fates really do know what they're doing here because I'm flying blind for the first time in a long time...

25

CONNOR

Ethan is awake!

Jack sent out a mass text message about fifteen minutes ago, so I'm rushing over to the house. I've spent the last week on the hunt for Doctor Douchenozzle after he somehow slipped out of the cells where Edward was holding him. He's been keeping himself in generic rooms and when he's been on the move, he's been blindfolded.

I can only assume the bitch of a goddess is the one helping him escape my observations. Considering she's supposedly the one who granted the abilities to the Sinclair line, it makes sense that she understands them well enough to render them moot. But I have to keep trying. I can't let this waste of space get his hands on my niece and nephews.

As I round the corner coming up on the house, I see Ric racing away.

That can't be good. For what reason would the Alpha be running *away* from his newly awakened mate and their children?

Pulling up to the house, I know something is very very wrong and I regret not following my Alpha. The shutters are down. The house is in lockdown. I don't even know who else is inside except for Ethan and the babies. I'm assuming Jack is there since he sent the text, but it's been radio silent since.

I try to call Jack but it goes straight to voicemail. Okay, so that means he's inside and the signal jammer is working... great.

Next attempt at a call is Max, but his goes straight to voicemail as well. I breathe a sigh of relief knowing that at least he is inside with everyone who matters to me...

Not everyone... well, maybe? I try Shaun's phone and it goes to voicemail. There's no way he could know I took his number from Ethan's phone and blocked it. Voicemail has my hopes up, but I have to be sure so I call the hospital. Savannah isn't on duty and neither is Shaun apparently, but the nurse didn't seem to know if he is in the building... just that he wasn't scheduled. A guy answers the line after I spend about fifteen minutes on hold.

"Yo! You got Mick aka Mouse aka greatest orderly known to man. How may I be of service today?"

Pulling the phone from my ear, I look down to make sure I called the hospital and not some sort of escort service before I respond, "This is Connor Sinclair. I need to..."

He cuts me off with a shushing noise and says, "Everyone is where they're supposed to be, which is NOT here. Trust yourself and those you love."

He hung up on me? I stare at my phone in confusion before another thought hits me. It's been a while since I've tried to reach out to Ethan with his mind speak, so I give it a try while pacing in the front yard.

Little brother? What's going on? I send out to him, hoping it reaches. It's not my ability to use so it's up to him to be listening to hear me.

Gear up, big brother. We're going to war, is the response I get back. War? What the fuck?

With who?! I send back to him. Who the fuck is worth going to war with when you've got newborns and just came back from the fucking dead?

The ones who made the mistake of fucking with me, he growls back and it somehow echoes through the pack.

Seb and Bastian come running up beside me, and we start the war council with the three of us on the front lawn and Max in the house with Ethan. It seems since giving birth, my baby brother has much better control over his abilities considering he set up a kind of mental conference room for us to discuss everything while he fades into the background.

Glancing through his eyes for a second, I see he's playing with his stuffies and I can't help but be thankful for that. Knowing that he's still able to be himself is a relief. Knowing that my boy is alright, I take the gamble and look through my mate's eyes.

I've avoided this since the day I laid him on that hospital bed; the day he thought he killed his best friend by leaving the room. I couldn't let him ever know that I was relieved he wasn't in that room when the gods showed up. They believed Josh was dead when they hit him because vampires can choose whether or not to have a heartbeat or breathe. They would have killed Shaun.

Not being in that room saved his life, but I couldn't let him see that in that moment. The guilt was already tearing him apart. I wasn't going to add survivor's guilt onto him as well.

Looking through his eyes, I see the sleeping babies. This is the first I've seen of them since their delivery. It's difficult to tear myself away, but I don't want to use Shaun's eyes for too long and cause him pain with the inevitable headache.

We need to figure out why Ric threw us into a lockdown, Max's thought brings me back to focus on the task at hand.

I get a text chime on my phone that pulls me away from the discussion. Looking at the message, I know something is very much wrong.

King Edward just informed me that Ric is under a psychic attack. We need to get organized. I'm calling Heartstone for backup, I send into our little conference while Seb and Bast start discussing who is going to start the evacuation procedures for the ones in our pack who can't or won't fight. Fucking cowards if they won't fight for their Alpha...

I will NOT ask a father to risk abandoning his family for the sake of my own family. No one is to be forced!

My little brother's voice rings in all our heads with some major oomph. His message holds the weight of an Alpha's authority, so I guess that answers that question...

"Connor? Is he really awake? I'm already on my way."

Bennet's voice snaps me back to the fact that I'm holding my phone up to my ear. I hurry to respond to him.

"Change of plans," I tell him. "He's up and good, but something psychic is attacking Ric so the house is on lockdown and our Alpha is off somewhere doing battle with the assistance of King Edward. Your son has declared war on the gods apparently and we're going to need some backup and a place of sanctuary for our innocent and noncombatants."

I finally take a breath and wait for the response... It seems to take forever before he replies.

"Send them to us. My men will be heading to you shortly. I'm going to be wherever my son needs me, so keep me apprised, Son."

I choke up a bit at being called "Son" by this man. It's been almost a decade since I've been called that, and I hadn't realized how much I missed having a father figure in my life.

As the call disconnects, I feel Ethan pounding in my head to get my direct attention.

Connie you hearing me?

What's up, Baby Blue? I send to him while I try to check in with the others. *Where'd Max go? He went silent in the middle of a sentence.*

I swear I hear the shadow of a giggle from my brother before he replies with *He's um... indisposed? Anyways, I need you to get Gramps to find Daddy like asap like fucking yesterday.*

At least I can give him a good piece of news here when I send back a reply.

Edward is already with Ric. They're trying to figure out who the witch is that's fucking with his head. As soon as they know who it is, they can bring in another to cast them out of him. They just need to make sure it's not a sympathetic or vengeance sworn family to the one fucking with the Alpha.

I can almost feel his relief at this piece of news, but I'm still kind of confused.

So, I kinda maybe sorta have a theory on who it is messing with Daddy's head, he sends to me. *Can you get a message to Gramps to jump to my mindlink? I'm not so good with the establishing a connection with the vamps yet unless they're really close by.*

Okay scratch the kind of. I'm really confused, but I send off the text message as requested.

> Ethan wants to talk to you. Says he has a theory on who is attacking Ric

Thumbs up emoji? Seriously? We're about to go to war with freaking gods and the response I get from the centuries old vampire is a fucking emoji...

We're screwed.

26

SHAUN

It takes hours before Ethan can convince Max and the others that they need to do a changing of the guard and get more people into the safety of the house and get some provisions inside. Unfortunately, that means that we have to rely on Connor to reveal where the release is for the office so we can get in there to unlock the house. By the time he's agreed to share the location with Max, I'm horribly strung out.

I had a migraine start a few hours ago that I can't figure out the cause of, and the babies are finally asleep again after Ethan and I moved them to the office for the extra layer of security. I understand the need for the caution, but to be honest, the only reason I'm even in this room is to avoid my mate who insisted he be one of the guards brought into the house. The babies are secondary to my own shame and avoidance right now.

A clicking noise has me looking up from staring at little Zander snoozing away. Ethan is standing at the desk and proceeds to turn the lock on the desk drawer. My sleep deprived brain takes too long to catch up to what he's just done, so I don't react in time.

"Sorry, bro!" he shouts before diving out of the window. I hear him hit the ground and let out a shout of my own before the shutters slam shut and the house is secure again.

"Asshole!"

Of course, between the house and my yelling, the babies are screaming and I'm crying, and it's all just too much. I can feel my grip on the magic inside slipping, my wolf is restless with the extra energy.

Need mate, he growls out to me. Yeah, buddy. I know we need him. But as usual, he's going to be too late.

I'm not exactly sure how long it takes, but Connor hits the release and comes tearing into the office to find me curled up on the floor rocking while all three babies are screaming bloody murder. He looks torn between rushing to me or assessing the babies, and ultimately the babies win out... of course they do.

Wait? *Am I jealous of babies now?*

I shake my head to clear it and pull out my phone from my pocket. Over the noise from the babies, I didn't even hear it ringing, but Ric is apparently calling me.

"What's up, Ric? You'll have to speak up," I practically need to shout into the phone to be heard and I can barely hear what he's asking me. Something about Felix and a possession and a broken neck?

"I wish there was something I could do, but even with magic I don't have the materials or ability to do the spells needed to heal a mortal injury like that," I try to explain to him. "A stab wound? Claw gash? Slashed throat? Those things are easy. Broken neck means both bones of the spinal column and brain stem affected. One miniscule mistake could mean paralysis or brain damage. I'm not confident enough to risk it."

"I believe you can do it," Connor's voice comes from behind me. "You are an amazing witch."

I don't know why I say it, but I hate him a little bit right now. He can't pull this shit with me right now. It's still too raw...

"Still not talking to you!" I snarl at him before going back to the call. "Sorry again, Ric. I'll ask around and see if we can find someone with the ability to heal that, but I don't think they'll make it in time."

As I hang up the phone, I see my mate disappearing through the door.

Way to go, Cleary.

Savannah comes in with a question on her face, but I wave her off to go wash my face in the bathroom. She closes and locks the door while I disappear into the temporary sanctuary. Letting the fresh tears fall, I pray to whatever is out there that we can fix this somehow. I'm just so fucking tired of being alone.

27

CONNOR

After leaving the office, I grab another cup of coffee. I can't help but wonder for the millionth time; how in the fuck am I an uncle to those three adorable babies? They are beautiful just like their papa was as a babe. I remember the day Mom and Dad brought him home and I fell in love. It's the same with these three.

Instantaneous love.

It was the same with Shaun, even though I didn't realize it at the time. I always liked it when he would gatecrash with Ethan at the diner. There was always something about the little shit that made me smile. Right around the time I turned eighteen, I started to feel jealous of my little brother, so I distanced myself.

When we lost Ethan, Shaun became a constant reminder of what I lost. It wasn't only when I saw him. It was like a shard of glass ripping through my chest every time I got an email, or a letter, or a voicemail... He didn't give up for over eight years. *My* hope crumbled and disappeared practically immediately, but Shaun never let me forget my failures.

Had I not ignored him, run from him, I would have known my mate years ago. Shaun has always been the one I love, and I don't deserve him.

You're right, son.

What in the fuck? I know it's been difficult this last year with reconciling who my mother actually was with the woman who raised me, but I didn't think it would make me go insane...

You aren't insane. I came back to you, my little love. The Goddess has given us a chance to make things right.

I know I shouldn't trust the Goddess after everything she put Ethan through, but for the longest time, she was his only solace. She came to his rescue in Atlanta, or so everyone says. I still feel the shame of not being there for him then. Maybe she is trying to make things right, like Mom says.

"What do you want, Mother?" I whisper staring at the floor.

Only to be a part of you again, my sweet boy. Mama knows best what is good for you. You have been miserable for too long now, and I'm going to make it all better now.

The thought of surrendering my pain to this woman, to my Mama, is tempting. In my conscious mind, I know it's absolutely wrong. This woman was a monster to an innocent baby for my entire life, and I never knew, never let myself see it. Letting her anywhere near any of us would be disastrous.

My mind knows this, but my heart falters for just a second.

That second is all she needs apparently. Suddenly it's like I'm stuck inside of my ability, only instead of looking and hearing out of someone else's head, it's my own. I am no longer in control of my body, speech, or actions.

Walking past Seb and Bastian, I'm screaming in my head that I'm not me. *They need to stop me!* My body is heading for the office where the babies are. I struggle and scream, but it does no good. My hand reaches up to knock on the door.

Please don't answer. Please keep me out. I don't know what she'll do. Please hate me enough to keep me out...

I hear the lock disengage and I try so hard to get my legs to turn away. I attempt to reach my wolf to shift us so we can run, but...He's not responding.

He can't seem hear me either. I've never felt fear like this before, but my body is calm, my heartbeat steady.

The door opens to reveal Savannah, the nurse from the Heartstone pack. I forgot Bennet sent her over to help out when I made the call earlier.

This is not good. She doesn't know me enough to know I'm not me. If even two of my closest friends didn't notice, how could a stranger?

She's saying something about the babies doing well, pointing out who is who, but I don't hear it. I vaguely recollect that the last she knew we couldn't figure out the names Ethan wanted to use for which babies, but it's irrelevant.

I can feel my mother's sinister aura rising inside of my body. She means to harm the babies, and there is nothing I can do to stop her.

The sound of the bathroom door opening pulls my attention away from the babies. Shaun emerges, wiping his hands on his pants and looks at me. I see disgust on his face fall away to be replaced with horror.

He sees it.

He knows she is here and in control.

My mate, even through his hatred of me, knows when I am not myself.

The brief flash of joy at his recognition brings my wolf to the surface, but he doesn't understand what is going on. Somehow, my mother has his instincts blocked, yet he senses my underlying fear and shifts us. I try to get through to him, make him understand, but it's like I'm shouting into the void.

We can't be shifted around the babies! They're too small! I cry out to him, desperate for him to hear me.

My wolf isn't hearing me. She's blinded, deafened him and he's feral. I am not in control. He is merely a wild beast on the loose in this locked room with my brother's three beautiful, innocent babies.

I scream and scream to whoever might hear me, hoping someone can stop me before it's too late.

Joshua! Edward! Ethan! Someone?

Stop me before I kill them all!

Savannah shifts first and although she's strong for a she-wolf, she's no match for the Beta of the pack. As my wolf knocks her out, he loses interest. I heave a sigh of relief that he decided not to kill her.

She would be a fine match for you if she was a higher ranking bloodline. My mother's voice sends a shiver through my spirit. My wolf isn't feral, not truly. My mother is guiding him, influencing him.

This is so much worse...

Shaun is suddenly between me and the bassinets.

"Connor, I need you to take back control," he whispers, maintaining eye contact with my wolf. "I can help, but I need you to be in this fight. You can't give up like you gave up on Ethan."

His words strike the final blow. The flash of guilt and pain are enough for my mother to wrest complete control and the last hold I had on my body is gone. I can do nothing but watch from the outside as my wolf rakes his claws down the side of our mate who is shielding our niece with his own body.

I'm trying to grab my wolf, to restrain him, but I have no physical form to get a grip on him. Something I'm doing must be working, or perhaps he senses I'm not with him, because the wolf backs away shaking his snout as if trying to dislodge something.

Or maybe? The thought brings me hope along with horror. The scent of our mate's blood is breaking through my mother's hold on him.

Shaun takes advantage and flings an arm out, using his magic to send my wolf through the window to the yard below. I watch mesmerized as my mate shifts into a beautiful dapple gray wolf. He is limping and the claw marks have barely stopped bleeding, but he glances my way before leaping through the opening to fight his mate.

I did that to him. I can't stop the disgust from flooding my system. A wolf cannot harm its mate. That is basic instinct. How the fuck did this happen?

If I can't bring you back, don't blame yourself. Maybe in the next life we can get an honest chance.

Did I just get a mind to mind message from Shaun? I thought only the vampires could do it.

Wait... Did he say next life?! No! No! No!

I force my spirit outside and see my wolf being tackled by Ric's midnight black wolf. Finally, there is someone here that can subdue me without getting injured. I fly toward my body and manage to make contact just as we hit the water of the pool. The shock of the water is enough to get me back inside.

Now, I just need to get control again.

Feeling a charm lay heavy over my chest, I know I've almost got it. I can't sense my mother at all, but I'm still not fully in the driver's seat. I'm not fully reintegrated with my body just yet. I need something else. I look for Shaun; he'll know what I need...

"No. No. No. No..."

He's not moving. I might have killed my mate. I tried to kill babies...

I leave my body again. I can't handle this. I tried to kill him.

You will do better. No son of mine will be with a half-breed mongrel.

In my despair, I drift farther away. I don't deserve this family. I'm only going to hurt them if I stay.

The world fades away to pure blackness, but my grief doesn't dissipate at all. It's only intensified.

"Well you aren't supposed to be here," says a somewhat familiar voice behind me.

Turning around, I'm thrown back to being five years old.

"Auntie Lizzie?!"

28

CONNOR

I'm in a weird empty space that I've never seen before and the woman in front of me reminds me so much of Ethan that I can't hold back the tears. How did I never make the connection before now? I knew in my head that his mother was named Elizabeth, but I never connected her with the teenager that used to babysit me and Ric when we were really young.

Maybe I didn't want to because that meant remembering that she took the beatings my grandfather wanted to put on me for not being enough of a man for him... at four years old.

"Sweet boy," she says to me, grabbing my chin and forcing me to look down into her face directly. "You turned into exactly the man you are supposed to be in spite of the nasty piece of work that my stepfather raised your mother to be."

Falling to my knees, I continue to look up at the woman who planted the seed of love and laughter in my heart at such a young age. If it hadn't been for her and Annabelle, I wouldn't know what love actually looks like. I'm back to being that little boy who only wants to be held and loved, before I had all of the responsibility thrust onto my shoulders...

I feel her arms around me, just as strong as they were when I was a child, filled with so much love.

"My son was lucky to have you as a brother, and you did beautifully, sweet boy," she whispers to me, stroking my back and soothing me through my sobbing. "He has others to protect him now. It's long past time for you to be the one who gets held, nurtured, and protected."

I pull away from her to see the sadness in her eyes.

"You were never meant to shoulder such a heavy burden, Connor. Let yourself be loved. Give up the control you don't want to wield anymore. It's time."

As I'm shaking my head, I feel her push me away. I don't want to leave her. She is the only light left in my life... if I'm even alive anymore...

You will be, sweet boy. Have faith in your love.

Next thing I know, I'm in my old suite inside the Alpha house, chained to the bed. Or rather, my body is. I'm still stuck outside of it. I go off in search of something or someone who can help and find my baby brother beating himself up over my situation.

Quit saying it's your fucking fault! It's my own damn fault... I tell him. *I don't know why I believed her when she said she wanted to help me be happy.*

I can tell I've lost his focus when the emotions showing on his face flutter from happy to sad to angry to... constipated?

Focus, little brother. I'm going to need you to grab the memory from me to show you what happened. I don't think I can say it and still manage to hold our connection. This whole witchblood thing they sprung on us isn't fair at all.

Yeah, that's another thing that I picked up on while trying to find someone to help me out here with the non-corporeal thing going on. Apparently, we're part witch through our maternal grandmother. I don't have all of the details, but that's apparently how my mother managed to hijack not only me, but Ric before me.

Ethan doesn't even give me a chance to explain anything, but rips the memory from me to understand what happened. At the end of it he races down the hall to my body. We apparently need to figure out how to get my consciousness, spirit, whatever to stay put inside my body before the sun comes up and I end up stuck as a ghost-ish thing like I am.

Edward shows up, followed by Celeste and Felix. Apparently, they expect me to go into Felix's body, so I know how to possess a body and then go into my own... Well, we give it a try and it's weird being fully inside someone else, not just their eyes and ears. Definitely not something I want to do ever again as I exit Felix's body to jump into my own. I don't like having control over someone else's actions...

I manage to open my eyes, but I can already feel the body trying to expel me. Whatever my mother did to me, it's going to kill me.

"It's not... going to hold. I'm sorry, Blue."

"No. No. No. No," Ethan keeps chanting it like a prayer through the tears he is struggling to hold back.

"You can't fight this for me, little brother," I whisper as a single tear rolls down to the pillow beneath my head. "Tell Shaun I'm sorry for me? Maybe now he can be happy again."

"Fuck you and your apologies, you self-centered alpha prick!"

I nearly cry in relief at the voice that growled into the room. My mate is alive. He is also barely standing, holding a bloody towel to his side and wearing a pair of sweats that are at least three sizes too big. But I didn't kill him...

Letting go of the doorframe, he almost crashes to the floor. Only Felix's quick reflexes manage to keep Shaun upright.

I can feel the hold on my body grow stronger with each step closer Shaun gets to the bed. I try to hold back the hope I'm feeling inside. I won't force anything on the man I almost killed less than two hours ago, no matter what it means for my own life.

"You have to bite him, Connie!" Ethan blurts out. "Bite him and we can all be family forever!"

The horror on my face is apparently funny to the little shit that I call my brother, but only because Shaun weakly shoves him out of the way with a chuckle of his own.

"Keep it down, Brat. We don't need the whole house to know," Shaun says weakly as he leans against the mattress before laying down next to me.

29

SHAUN

I finally regain consciousness after what Zach told me was about an hour. Everyone was worried because I stayed in my wolf form for so long, but that's actually pretty normal for me when I'm injured as a wolf. It keeps the magic contained while I'm not in control... something we came up with right after our first shift to keep the secret of what we are.

The downside to staying wolf while injured? They treated the wounds on the wolf side and shifting back to human opened them up again, at least enough to start bleeding. I hurried to the dresser in the room I was placed in to grab a pair of sweats and the towel off the top to staunch the blood. Looking down at the gashes, they're pretty gnarly and I'm pretty sure I'm getting my first grownup scar out of today.

Leaning against the furniture, I can feel my magic pulling me elsewhere in the house.

He needs you.

There's that voice again. I'm not normally one to put stock in creepy disembodied voices, but something about this lady's voice reminds me of my bestie and I trust him with everything in the entire universe.

Rushing as much as my injury will allow, I make it to the Beta suite to hear that Connor is giving up. I don't' hold back my growl, even though my injury is starting to make me a bit delirious. I don't even know what I'm saying, but Ethan is practically throwing me at his brother urging him to give me the claiming bite.

I chuckle at the way he's slipped down into his little personality but can't ignore the fact that the thought of claiming me seems to bring nothing but fear and disgust to my mate. I have to lay down or else fall down, so I park myself next to Connor and try to talk some sense into him.

"If this is what it takes to save your ass, you need to do it," I whisper to him. I can't live in a world without him in it. Even if he hates me, ignores me, rejects me... I don't care. He has to live.

"I won't allow my mother to force anyone to do anything ever again," he whispers back, his lips brushing across my forehead. "She doesn't get to do that anymore, not while I have any say in it."

So, he sees it as his mother forcing him to be with his mate? Nice to know where I rate in things. Apparently sticking it to his dead mother is more important than his own life, his brother, or his family... let alone me...

"You need to live!" I urge. I'm not brave enough to tell him that *I* need him to live, so I use the one person I know he actually does love. "Ethan won't survive losing you."

I won't survive losing you...

"We got less than five minutes until sunrise, so whatever you're doing you gotta do it now," Ethan calls out, not even bothering to hide his anxiety.

"I'm not sealing the bond when we don't know if it will even work!" Connor shouts, showing more animation than he has since I've met him as an adult, if I'm being honest. His voice is barely a whisper as he mumbles, "I can't be the reason you die as well. Bonded mates never survive the death of the other."

I grab him by the chin and use every ounce of what little strength I have left to force him to meet my gaze. My injury is taking a huge toll on me.

"We are fated," I tell him forcefully. "The bite is just to tie our bodies together. Our souls were linked from birth."

Connor manages to pull his face from my hands and stares at the wall... "I won't kill you..."

Looking at the clock, we're running out of time. Ethan is bouncing in anxiety with his thumb is in his mouth. Felix grabs his other hand, and they are holding on to each other for dear life.

Ethan's thoughts are leaking. He is begging Connor to just do it.

Why does he want to leave us? Why doesn't he want to be part of my family anymore?

My magic surges forward in response to my desperation and for once, my wolf doesn't even attempt to hold it back. My growl shakes the room, possibly the whole house, and I hear the babies waking up somewhere above us as a result.

"IF YOU WON'T DO IT, THEN I WILL!"

The magic rides me hard as I wrench Connor's head to the side to give my wolf the opportunity to latch onto his neck. The blood is sweet and his scent that reminds me so much of happier times intensifies. My wolf's euphoria is overshadowed by the realization of what I've just done.

This is what it feels like to be violated by choice...

The room is silent as I stand back up, wiping the little trace of blood from my chin with the back of my hand. Looking down at the man in the bed, I feel a deep shame that I've never felt before in my life. I can't be in here any more...

I exit the room as quickly as my injury will allow. I can't look at him anymore. I can't see them all being happy when I want to throw up from the rejection of my mate. I can actually *feel* his disgust inside of me from what I just did to save his life.

He's disgusted by me.

From the hallway, I take the time to mutter, "You'll live, you bastard. At least you'll live."

The world is turning a shade of grey and I try to fight it off long enough to find somewhere to collapse in my grief. I just tied myself to someone who doesn't want me, and there's nothing I can do to change that fact. The ramifications of my decision keep circling in my brain.

I vaguely notice there are others in the kitchen, but when Ric puts his arm around me to hold me upright, I realize I need something to boost my energy before everyone finds out what I've done, how low I've sunk...

The next wave of grief turns out to be too much as my legs completely give out under the strain. I can't hold back the tears anymore. I feel myself laid down on a soft surface and just let the pain consume me.

30

CONNOR

It's been almost six months since the big battle against the gods, and life in the Jameson pack is probably the best it's ever been since Ric's grandfather was the Alpha. If only my personal life was in as good of shape as the pack, it would be perfect.

After the fighting, I hurried home to take a shower and clean up before looking for my mate. Apparently, that extra thirty minutes was too long of a delay because I haven't seen him since the pre-battle strategy session where he used his magic to protect us all. The shame and disgust I felt for myself back then was deserved. How fate thought someone as selfless and wonderful as Shaun deserves someone as useless as me is a mystery.

Since the day that he tied himself to me, I've been striving to make myself worthy of him as a mate. Suffice it to say, there was a lot of work to be done when I came home after the post battle celebrations. The memory of that first realization still comes to me when I look back.

He left us, my wolf whimpers in my mind.

Looking around the living room, I can't say that I blame him. It's deplorable...

There are takeout containers and dirty dishes everywhere in sight. Mail is piled up on every surface. Dirty clothes litter the room...

And what the fuck is that smell?!?

No wonder my mate ran. I'm not anywhere near good enough for him.

But he claimed us, my wolf reminds me.

Yes, he did. And it's about time I make sure it wasn't a mistake on his part. We will become worthy of him. We won't show him this pathetic version ever again. The man and wolf he meets the next time he sees us will be completely different.

Agreed, *growls my wolf as a new sense of determination takes root. Shaun deserves a better man and I am going to be better for him.*

Pulling into the parking lot of the hospital, I know I'm not there yet, but I can't go another day without seeing him. It's been difficult keeping my wolf from hunting him down, but even he agrees that our mate deserves the best version of us after I royally screwed everything up. And I have to admit, Valentine's Day is a good excuse to reunite with my mate.

As I scan the lot, I don't see Shaun's car. After Ethan forced us all to binge watch the entirety of Supernatural a few months ago, I understand the obsession with the car; however, I wouldn't waste the money or effort on a classic like that unless I had another mode of transportation... Shaun is lucky that he hasn't ended up stranded in the mountains yet.

I guess I should have double checked to make sure he would be working today, but I figured since he wasn't at the Alpha house that Shaun would be working. Considering I never got the opportunity to get Shaun's number for myself, I send a text to my baby brother to find out if he knows where my mate is...

> U hear from your BFF lately? He's not at his work.

It takes about five minutes for me to get a response, and it makes me race away from the hospital toward the interstate as fast as my truck can go. I just hope I can catch up to him.

He got a call from his mom early this morning
and took off in a hurry.

Once I'm on the highway headed for the interstate, I call my baby bro to try and get a direction in which to go. I don't remember much about his parents, but Mr. Morrison, Jack's teacher, told us that they basically abandoned Shaun at college when he was just fifteen years old. The guilt of leaving my mate alone to fend for himself all of those years still eats at me, but it's not like I can go back...

"Connie, what's wrong?" Ethan asks as the call connects. The suspicion in my brother's voice reminds me that I haven't exactly been the best brother, mate, friend, or hell... human... for the last year or so.

"Why are you looking for Shaun now? You aren't going to do something stupid like try to reject the mate bond, are you?"

I end up fishtailing around a corner in my surprise.

"Have I really been that much of an ass?" I ask out loud.

The giggle on the other end confirms it and I can't help the smile that breaks through my worry. I'll never get used to hearing that sound. The growl that erupts from my chest reminds me that I have a reason for this call and my attention snaps back to the task at hand.

Ethan's giggle cuts off at the sound of the growl.

"Did you just growl at my boy?" Ric's voice booms over the line. I guess I didn't realize I was on speakerphone...

"Wasn't me," I breathe out as I take another sharp turn. I'll be at the interstate in about two miles and need a direction. "My wolf was just reminding me we're in a rush. Where would Shaun be heading if he's heading to his mother? I'm on the road trying to catch up to him."

"I'll have to call Edward to find out where they settled. They were nomads after they left here from what I've seen in the pack records," Ric says after a second. "I'll check with his people and see what they know." To Ethan, he adds, "I'm going to head to the office, baby boy. You good until the trips get up?"

I pull off at the gas station by the interchange to fill up on my tank. Until I have a destination, I'm stuck here.

"I'm good, Daddy," I hear my brother say away from the phone and pointedly ignore the sounds of what is probably a rather steamy goodbye kiss by the sound of it. It takes me a minute to realize they forgot I'm on the line, so I clear my throat and try to erase the thoughts of my best friend and little brother being intimate.

The line goes dead on me and I stare at it incredulously. Did the little shit just hang up on me? I'm desperate to find my mate! Doesn't he know something must be extremely wrong for Shaun to go looking for his parents?

Sorry, Connie. I don't want Daddy to listen in on this.

Ethan's voice flits into my head as I start filling up the tank on my truck. *What do you know and why don't you want your Alpha to know?* I send back to him wondering why he's keeping secrets from Ric.

My bestie isn't pack yet, so it's not his business. But since you've finally got your head out of your ass about him, I might be nice and share some information with you.

I can hear the growl of my brother's wolf through the mind link connection, and I can feel the supplication of my own wolf. I'm not sure if it's because he's a true Alpha Mate or if it's because of his convoluted bloodlines, and at this point I don't think I care. I'll bow down to anyone if it means finding my mate faster.

Tell me what you know, Blue. I can feel something is wrong and I need to get to him.

I hear the echo of a sigh of relief in my head and then Ethan sends over some information that has my heart skipping a beat.

His father is gone and his mother called to tell him that she's coming here for him. I don't think she meant it in the way that she wants to be a mommy to him finally. He ran out of here and gunned it like his ass was on fire. I told Daddy he got called in to work for an emergency to give him time to get away.

My mind is reeling with this information. His mother is the reason he's panicking?

Ethan, this is important. Do you know where he's running to?

The pause before a response makes me wonder if my baby brother got distracted.

Sorry, Alec had another blowout and Daddy just happened to be holding him this time. I can't stop laughing...

I take a second to peek through Ethan's eyes to get a glimpse of the sight and sure enough, there is the big bad Alpha, covered in baby shit. We all told him that the so-called blowout barrier advertised on the diaper packages would never hold up to Alec...

I'm still wiping the tears from my eyes from laughing so hard when Ethan continues.

All I know is that he got his usual Christmas card from his father, like usual, and it was postmarked from New Orleans this time. If she's coming from there, he got out of here with at least a nine hour head start.. at least as long as she wasn't already on the road.

That gives me the direction I need. I'm going to head north and hopefully catch up to him. If he's running away from her, he'd need to go north...

I'm going to get to I-95 north and find him. His Impala isn't in good enough shape to outrun my truck.

Hell, I think that car burns through gas faster than my truck, honestly.

Good luck, Cun-Cun!

I feel the connection with Ethan snap after he uses my old nickname from when he was a toddler. It snaps me back to reality in a way that nothing else would at this point. I failed one boy. I'm not failing my mate.

31

SHAUN

Having an older car is nice in the winter when it comes to getting traction in the snow, but I really should have made fixing the heater more of a priority before now. Between the faulty heating element and the back window that isn't sealed properly, I'm freezing as I pull off into a truck stop in Pennsylvania. I need to check my funds and figure out where I'm going to go from here.

I took I-95 up to Baltimore and then realized I was headed for the one place my mother drilled into my father that we couldn't go. Ellicott City is bigger than where I've been living, but there's something there that my mother was running from my whole life. I didn't even realize I was driving there until I got off of I-95 and got onto I-70 and saw the exit signs. I drove right past and stayed on I-70 West and now I'm in this major truck stop town, needing to come up with my next destination.

Instinct pulled me to Ellicott City, which is where I don't want to be. I need another destination...

Not instinct, my wolf tells me. *Magic calls blood.*

Great... My mother's insanity is pulling me in.

I dig my phone out of the pocket of my backpack that I threw on the front seat only to realize it didn't charge at all for the entire drive. I thought the issue was the charging cord, but apparently my port in the car has given up on me as well. Looking around from the gas pumps where I'm shivering, I see a couple of options for a hotel room, but I need off the radar. Asking the clerk inside, I find out there's a motel just past the on-ramp for the toll road.

I thank him and go back into the cold to make the drive over. Anonymity is more important than comfort right now. I need a decent shower, electricity to charge my phone, and time to plan... Once I have a plan in place, I'll know if I need to buy a decent coat or not...

I'm starting to appreciate how effortless my father made this seem when I was a kid. I spent so long resenting my parents for uprooting me all of the time, but now that I'm doing it myself...

The old man at the office of the motel doesn't even look at me. He just asks for fifty dollars cash and slides me a room key... like an actual key. Any hope of Wi-Fi just went out the window as I grab the key and head to the room he assigned me. Pulling the Impala right up in front of the door for a quick getaway, I don't even turn the key when the car sputters and dies.

Don't do this to me, baby...

I try for a half an hour to get the car to start again, just so I know it will, but it won't even click anymore. I'm now stuck in some truck-stop town motel in Pennsylvania with fate only knows what after me...

My mother was right... I can't run from this...

Six Hours Earlier

"No fair!" Ethan whispers as I successfully get all three babies to sleep at the same time. According to everyone in the house, I'm the only one with the magic touch. I keep telling them I'm not using magic to do it, but they don't believe me.

We're both still chuckling as we enter the kitchen, Ethan with the baby monitor on a lanyard around his neck, right next to the clip for his binkie.

But for now, he's still in his adult headspace. He'll regress into his little headspace when Ric gets done in the office and can play with him.

But for now? Coffee...

I just got off a twelve hour shift in the ER and was half hoping I would catch Connor at the house today. It's Valentine's Day after all and I'm tired of the game of hide and seek we've been doing for the last six months.

At first the pain of his rejection was too much to bear, so I hid away and worked my ass off, taking every possible shift and banking all of my PTO. Ethan recruited Mick and Zach to force me away from the hospital about three months ago for a "friendsgiving" feast. Although we were all invited to actual Thanksgiving, being fully catered after last year's debacle, both Mick and I had to work the holiday.

After the holiday meal, my friends started to drag me out of my funk more and more to the point where I started staying over in the Jameson pack again. I was still hiding from my mate, but at least I was giving fate more of a chance to push us back together. I could still feel an echo of how he was feeling, but it was growing weaker the longer we were apart.

My phone ringing makes both of us jump and Ethan rushes toward me to silence the offending device. I hold it away from his reach lest he actually try to break my phone and accidentally hit answer before looking to see who it is.

"Shaun Eliazor Cleary!"

FUCK!

Ethan looks like he's seen a ghost and I'm suddenly not in the mood for coffee. I'm not in the mood for anything but getting this woman off the phone as quickly as possible.

"What do you want, Mother?" I ask in as nice of a manner that I can possibly manage for the woman who treated me like a piece of luggage my whole life, until my being gay and into lingerie, and unwilling to give up the fact that my best friend was suffering and we could help him....

"I'm coming for you," she says, breaking my chain of thought. "Your father is gone, and the wolf's warding is lifted from me. They know where I am now, and I need you."

Part of me is pleased that my mother is admitting to needing me, but her next words tank even that small bit of hope.

"This is why you were born. I needed a backup plan for when I lost your father. You can't run from this, boy."

I hang up the phone before she can say another word. The rage I'm feeling... I have to get out of here. I have to get away from Ethan, from the babies, from my mate... She will destroy everything good to get me under her thumb, the same way she broke down my father over the years.

In the back of my mind, it registers that Ethan is calling after me, but my tires kick up gravel against the house.

"Goodbye," I whisper to the men in the doorway as they grow smaller in my rearview mirror. "I love you. Please don't let him suffer for me."

Wiping the tears from my eyes, I grab my backpack from the passenger seat. There's nothing else I can do right now except go in the room. I'll freeze in the car. If I can't get it to start again in the morning, I'll just have to hitch a ride the old fashioned way...

32

CONNOR

It's just by chance that I noticed the Impala before taking the ramp for the toll road. I don't know how long he's been at the motel, but now that I've found him, Shaun isn't getting away from me. I pull up next to the car and notice the back passenger window is cracked. Feeling the hood, it's still warm-ish. That at least lets me know that he hasn't been here long.

I don't waste time grabbing anything but my phone out of the truck before I race to the door in front of the car. I consider announcing myself, but not being certain of what kind of reception I'll receive, I don't want to risk being turned away. I knock...

The door cracks open before I can even put my hand back down and the only thing I notice about Shaun is that he's been crying.

Who hurt mate? My wolf growls in my head.

The fact that it was probably his own mother is something I can sympathize with, but I don't ever want to see this kind of pain on my mate's face.

"Connor? Is it really you?" he asks softly. I nod and give him a soft smile, hoping that I'm not going to get a door slammed in my face. It's fucking cold out here and knowing he's been crying; I will do anything to make him smile.

Before I can react, he grabs my shirt and pulls me inside, slamming me up against the now closed door. He may be shorter than me, and a beta wolf, but he is all dominance right now. I will submit anything to this man, if only he will smile for me again.

"Help me forget," he snarls into the side of my neck before latching onto the scar of his bite from six months ago. The pull of his mouth connects directly to my crotch and I feel myself reacting, getting ready for whatever he wants.

"Use me," I breathe out, lifting my chin up to give him better access. "I'm yours. However you need me, any way you want me. Only yours."

Shaun steps back just enough to glance at my face before I'm thrown to the bed by an unseen force. I watch my mate stalk toward me from the door, and I feel only excitement. Part of me wonders if he is still a virgin, like he told his friend at the cabin, but in reality, I don't care. I want this man inside of me... or on top of me... I don't care which. I just want him.

I attempt to sit up to start removing my clothing, but I'm slammed back onto the bed. My arms are yanked above my head, almost as if they are tied there. I hear a chuckle from next to the bed and see Shaun looking down at me with a hunger I've never seen on any man's face before, at least not for me.

I can only watch my mate climb up on the bed next to me and reach for the button of my jeans. I notice his hands trembling, but the invisible bindings on my wrists mean I can't help him with this.

"Relax, sweetheart," I say. "You have me forever."

He meets my eyes and I can see his nerves warring with his hunger. I want to hold him, comfort him. Yet at the same time, I want him to tear me apart and destroy me. It's a feeling I've never had before. I've always assumed I had to be the one to be in charge, being born an alpha. However, giving up control to my mate isn't even a question. He rules over me completely...

As Shaun sits back on his heels to take a few breaths, I have to clarify my previous statement. "You have me forever, but I don't think my dick got that memo. I need you, Shaun. I need my mate to take me, unravel me, break me..."

Before I can say another word, Shaun silences me with a kiss. And this isn't just your run of the mill smooch. Calling it a kiss is like calling the Mona Lisa a portrait. While technically true, it fails to capture the sheer magnificence of the thing. This kiss is the Sistine Chapel of kisses. It's purely divine...

33

SHAUN

Connor found me.

Connor wants me.

My magic kind of took over for a minute and now I have my mate, *my extremely virile and sexy mate*, magically bound to a bed in a seedy motel room and I can't stop kissing him. Should I tell him he's my first kiss?

Hell, he's my first everything. I'm terrified of doing something wrong. He has to be so much more experienced than I am and it's going to be painfully obvious that I don't know what I'm doing. Books can only take you so far...

He's ours, my wolf reassures me. *Instinct will show the way.*

I decide to trust my wolf in this. After all, he's the one that pulled Connor into the room. Trust my instinct? I can do that... maybe.

I collapse onto Connor's chest and just listen to his heartbeat while I try to get out of my head enough to make this enjoyable for him. His heart is racing just as much as mine is... Does this mean he wants me as much as I want him?

"Sweetheart," Connor's voice rumbles beneath my cheek. "Please do something. Kiss me, suck me, fuck me... I don't care which. But please don't leave me like this. I *need* you."

Looking up into his eyes, I see it. He has given his everything to me in this moment. Glancing down his body, I see the rather large situation below his waist. Oh, boy. I want it.

Sitting up on my knees, I half crawl over his lap so that I can get his jeans unbuttoned. I'm not sure if it's my own strength or my magic, but his pants go flying across the room, knocking over the single chair for the table in the room. His boxer briefs follow suit a few seconds later and I'm seeing the most glorious penis I've laid eyes on outside of porn.

Okay, to be honest, the human penis looks like an alien coming out of a balloon animal. None of them look *good* per say, but I still find myself wanting to swallow Connor's down until my nose touches his body...

Note to future self: work up to deep throating...

I'm gagging and coughing, trying not to throw up on my mate while he makes some sort of crooning noise. At least he's not laughing at my incompetence...

"Build up to it, baby," he whispers. "Any touch from you is more than I ever hoped to get."

Alright, that is some sweet stuff there. Instead of trying to go all porn star on him this time, I decide to start by licking. From the noises he's making and the way my magic is flaring with every pull he makes against his bonds, I can only assume he's enjoying it. As his pleasure grows, I notice mine does as well.

The idea hits me, and I need to act on it immediately. I climb off the bed to a sound of desperation from Connor. Oh, how I want to recreate that sound many times over...

Under his heated gaze, I start removing my own clothing. As I remove my shirt, I see the wince when the latest scars on my torso are revealed. Before the fire is completely banked in his gaze, I grab his nape and pull him into another heated kiss.

"That was your bitch of a mother's fault," I growl at him. "We both lived through it. Now get out of your head so that I can get my dick in your mouth."

His shock at my words seems to be enough to get us back on track, so I back away again to give him a full view while I unbutton my own jeans. Sliding the zipper down reveals a hint of lace, so I try to keep it covered with my hand. I'll just pull my underwear down with my jeans and then I won't have to worry about his reaction.

I can wear regular underwear again. I can give it up for him...

"Are you wearing something pretty?"

I jump at the words growled from the man on the bed. Does he know? How could he know?

In my shock, I let go of my jeans and they slide off my hips to reveal the teal lace jock covering my no longer hard penis. I'm laid bare, and it's scaring the shit out of me. I don't know what to do. My heart is pounding in my ears. I can see Connor saying something, struggling against my magic to get up, but I can't hear him.

Being rejected again is something I can't handle...

I hurry to put my clothes back on. Connor is increasing his struggles on the bed. He's not erect anymore either. I knew it. I disgust him.

Somehow, I manage to get outside the room fully dressed and I'm inside the Impala before I remember that my baby died on me. I can't be here anymore. I just can't face him.

My magic surges up, outside of my control, and there's only one thought in my mind.

Let me be anywhere but here, somewhere I'm wanted...

34

SHAUN

A strange hotel room is not where I expected to be waking up. My first thought is that my panic attack caused me to black out and Connor took me to a nicer place to sleep it off. Not only am I not that lucky, but the biggest clue to negate that thought is the fact that I can't scent him at all, not even on me. Even without him carrying me, my clothes should still smell like him from how up close and personal we were, but there's not even a trace.

Looking down at my body, I see that the clothes I'm wearing are *not* mine. I don't wear anything other than t-shirts, hoodies, or scrub tops since I graduated from med school. The last time I wore a shirt with buttons was my interview at the hospital, and I know I didn't pack that to run away.

"You look good in your father's suit."

The sound of that voice brings nothing but dread. Groaning, I realize my mistake. I thought about needing to be somewhere I was wanted, but I know better than to be less than specific with magic. Of course, my mother wants me. She wants to use me. She doesn't want her son. She wants her backup plan.

"Where am I, Mother?" I ask, sitting up and rubbing my temple. It wasn't only my own magic that brought me here.

Not our magic at all, my wolf supplies. *Witches pulled us by force.*

That is not a comforting thought. If she's working with other witches...

My wolf's growl rumbles through the hotel room as I repeat the question, "Where AM I?"

She flinches at the growl, but is otherwise nonplussed when she responds, "We're a few miles from my childhood home. It's time you meet your grandfather."

It's not a stretch to understand why her words fill me with unease. My parents never talked about their own parents. I always assumed they were gone, but apparently, I should have asked more questions growing up. Without my dad around, I'm now at the mercy of my mother and her family, and it scares the shit out of me. If this woman was raised to be so callous toward her own flesh and blood, what can I expect of the man who raised her?

"Of course, I had to make sure you were presentable," she rambles on, her confidence growing with my silence. "None of that *perverse* clothing is acceptable. You are a man, and it's time you do your duty and produce an heir for the blood. It is what is demanded of you as a witch."

I'm trying to follow along, but so far the only thing I'm understanding is the fact that my mother magically kidnapped me to bring me to my grandfather, and she got rid of my clothing for the boring ass uncomfortable shit that I'm wearing now. There's something not right with what she's telling me, but I don't know how to decipher what it could be aside from fearing my grandfather.

"Hurry up, boy!" she yells from the now open doorway. The wind coming into the room isn't as cold as it was in Pennsylvania, but it is definitely colder than back home. I have a bad feeling about where we are and reach for my magic to try and do that little teleport trick in reverse, but I don't get any response. My magic isn't gone, but it's like it is locked away, out of my reach.

"Yes, I bound your magic," Mother says as she grabs my arm to drag me out the door. "I can't have you screwing this up for me, too. Now that your father isn't here, there's nothing stopping me from being free."

With that cryptic remark, the woman throws me into the backseat of an older SUV and slams the door. Fuck waiting around to find out what is going on. I throw myself at the door and pull the handle... nothing happens. I slide across to the other door... again nothing. The child safety locks must be engaged.

I try to jump to the front seat but get thrown back by magic. Someone put warding inside of this vehicle for this very reason. I know it's pointless, but I try to climb over the back to attempt the hatch. The force of the magic keeping me in the backseat seems to shrink down on me, pushing me into the cushions the more I struggle against it. It doesn't take long for the magic to have me immobilized completely prone across the backseat.

My mother climbs into the driver's seat as soon as I can no longer fight back... typical cowardice. She doesn't even have the decency to look at me before she starts the drive. I can only glimpse parts of the road signs from where I'm bound by her magic, but it quickly becomes obvious that we're in the only place I knew I didn't want to be... Ellicott City.

My panic starts to rise again, but the sound of a phone vibrating pulls me back. I need to concentrate. I need to find a way out of this so that I can get back to my mate...

Shit! Connor. Did he ever get free? Did whatever my mother pull leave him alone? Did my magic just dissipate or is he still bound by it while I'm not in control of my magic?

"Rebecca, you were warned never to return," a stern man's voice comes through the speakers. "Without David, there is no reason for you to be here. Turn around before we are forced to take action."

I want to ask what is going on, but whatever magic my mother has used to contain me has also robbed me of my voice. My mother always made it seem like she was running from here. Now, it appears that she was not only *not welcome* here, she also used a fake name. Is her real name Rebecca?

"David is gone, Dad," she says as she turns off the main road. From what I can see and feel, we're heading up a rather steep climb. "I'm not here for you, but if you hurry you might actually get to meet your grandson."

"*You don't get to call me that,*" the voice on the phone growls, powerful enough to make my wolf take notice.

He is Alpha of his pack, my wolf tells me. *We are trespassing.*

This is most definitely not good. I didn't spend the last three years as a lone wolf without knowing the necessary laws and restrictions that come with being one. My mother bringing me into their pack territory without permission is grounds for them to execute me on site. She gets apprehension. I get a death sentence... The howls in the air mean I'm fucked...

Before the panic can even take hold, the vehicle skids to a stop and the door behind me is thrown open. Thanks to the spell, I can't even move to lift my chin and see who opened it. But I smell them. Fae.

As if this day isn't bad enough...

35

CONNOR

Shaun was terrified.

That's the only thing that keeps running through my head. The only thing that has ever ripped out my heart worse than being forced to stay here while he was panicking was when my mother took control of my body, causing me to almost kill him. I have an idea what might have set him off, but until I can find him, I can't be sure. I was stupid to mention his underwear. I should have just enjoyed the view...

As soon as the door to the room closed behind him, I was free from his magical bondage. I grabbed my pants and yanked them on as quickly as I could, but it wasn't fast enough. I yank the motel room door open only to watch helplessly while my mate disappears in front of my eyes. He was right there, in the front seat of his car, but I doubt he could see me through his tears. His magic took him away from me. Without the car, I have no idea where he could be...

My phone ringing stops my emotions from spiraling out of control. The only thought running through my head is that Shaun didn't mean to disappear and he wants me to come get him. Yeah, that makes sense. I hurriedly swipe to answer the call without looking at the name on the screen.

"Con-man, you there?" Ric's voice comes through before I can get it up to my ear. "I may have a lead on where Shaun could be headed."

"I lost him, Ric," I tell him, barely holding back my despair. Of course he didn't call. He doesn't know my number..."He just fucking disappeared on me."

My best friend is silent on the other end of the call while I slide down the side of my truck to rest with my back against the front tire. Even though the temperature is in the teens and dropping with the sun starting its descent, I don't feel the cold. I just feel numb.

I'm staring at the wheel well of Shaun's Impala when I notice something. Thanks to Ethan's insistence of watching every single episode of Supernatural, I recognize what I believe to be a hex bag tucked up in there. Knowing my mate would never do anything to possibly damage his car, regardless of how much of a piece of shit it currently is, I can only guess that another witch did something to his car.

Ric was apparently talking while I was inspecting the Impala, so I grab the bag and try to focus back on the phone call. Until I can find a witch, I'll have to leave the magic be for the moment.

"...was like a son to the Alpha when he took off, so if Shaun knows about it he might go there," Ric says.

I shake my head to clear it because something is making my head all kinds of fuzzy right now.

"I need a witch," I manage to slur out. My vision is starting to go grey around the edges. This has something to do with that hex bag. "Shaun... taken... witch..."

I vaguely hear Ric yelling on the other end of the phone, and I barely manage to climb up into the cab of the truck before the world completely greys out.

A knock on the window jolts me awake with a growl. Neither I nor my wolf appreciate the malicious magic that was used on our mate and us. I can barely contain the beast inside until I look behind me to see it was King Edward himself knocking on my window. Somehow, I manage to clamber out of the passenger side without making an even bigger fool of myself.

"Connor Sinclair," he greets me as he comes around the front of my truck. "What have you done to get tangled up in this mess with the witches?"

The confusion on my face must be as obvious to him as his is to me because he then follows up with another question that makes me really worry as to what is happening.

"Let's go with an easier question. Why are you here and not back at your own pack playing with and protecting my grandson and great-grandbabies?"

At my look of incredulity, he just raises a single golden eyebrow, waiting for an answer.

"I came after my mate," I tell him. "Didn't you give Ric information on where he might be headed?"

The vampire just stares at me for a long while... long enough that I completely understand why they freak people out when they forget to breathe or blink.

His phone alert goes off and he finally moves to check the screen. The frown on his face doesn't reassure me at all, especially when he proceeds to move his fingers across the screen. For the six hundred year old vampire king, he should be able to use the mind speaking ability with anyone in his kingdom or family, so why is he needing to resort to texting?

"Relax, Connor," he says without looking up from his phone. "I try to not intrude on other's minds without their permission unless it's an emergency." He mutters some more under his breath. I think he says something along the lines of "especially not old wolves who can make even my life difficult."

I still don't have any clue what he's talking about, but I need to find out what Ric was saying so that I can go after Shaun. I can feel his fear. Wherever he is, he is afraid. My wolf doesn't like it... neither do I.

My phone starts ringing from within the truck. Before I go to answer it, I look to Edward for permission. I know better than to ignore him without Ethan around. If not for Ric and Alpha Heartstone, this vampire would have killed both me and my mate last year just because Shaun is a hybrid.

At the vampires nod, I grab the phone and see this time it's Ethan calling. As soon as the call connects, I can hear the babies screaming in the background, along with what sounds like Seb, Bast, and Max trying to get them to calm down...

"Connie? Did you find him?" Ethan's frantic voice comes over the speaker loud enough to catch Edward's attention. "Cassie just showed up and said you need to be with him within the hour or I lose my bestie. Don't let me lose him! Don't let me lose *you!*"

I haven't even been able to say a word, but my baby brother is bawling his eyes out on the phone and his grandfather is shooting daggers at me with his gaze. Tearing my eyes away from the vampire, it hits me what was said... an hour? How in the hell can I get to him within an hour when I don't even know where he is?

"Little wolf, calm yourself," Edward says loud enough to carry over the phone. I hear the sobbing cut off abruptly with a hiccup. "I will help your cousin find his mate. You won't lose them."

The reminder that Ethan isn't my brother is like another stab to my battered heart. There's not much more it can take before it crumbles away completely...

"MY *BROTHER* will find his mate with or without your help, *King Edward,*" a cold voice resembling Ethan's comes out of the speaker. "You would do well to remember who it is that was there for me my whole life, who mourned the loss of me, who taught me what familial love is. Because it sure as hell wasn't any fucking vampire who did those things."

The phone call disconnects and I'm at a loss for words. Never in a million years did I expect Ethan to defend me like that. Yes, I'll always view him as my baby brother but I thought he was only still calling me brother out of habit. Looking up at the vampire, I see a smirk on his face. It's not exactly instilling hope that he's going to assist me.

"Well, Connor," the vampire says. "Looks like I'm going to be helping you get to your missing mate."

Before I can respond, I'm grabbed and moving faster than I ever have before. The closest I've ever come to even a fraction of this speed is on the Ducati that Ethan got me last Christmas. When we stop, it takes a few seconds for my stomach to catch up to the rest of my body.

Vamp speed is no joke. I double over to take some deep breaths, praying that my insides *remain* on my inside...

"Eddie, what are you doing in my territory unannounced?" comes a growling voice from in front of me. "And who's the pup?"

I lift my head and immediately fall to my knees in surprise. The Alpha in front of me is probably the most powerful wolf alive based on what I'm sensing through my wolf, and yet he barely looks to be fifty years old. With age comes power, so for a wolf to have the power I can sense from this man, he should be at least one hundred.

"One hundred seventy five, but who's counting," mutters Edward in response to my thoughts.

I thought you don't intrude without permission? I think at him.

The wolf in front of me laughs and the sound strikes a chord of familiarity in me. I know that laugh, or at least an echo of it. I can't stop myself from blurting out, "You're related to Shaun."

The room goes silent.

"How do you know my grandson?" the old wolf growls at me, and I wonder, not for the first time, why fate has me surrounded by the most powerful fucking beings in our world.

36

SHAUN

"You promised us a witch, Rebecca," the fae who appears to be in charge sneers at my mother as she is kneeling before him on the ground. "You owe us after we boosted your love spell on David."

HOLD THE FUCK UP?!

Even if I wasn't still immobilized by my mother's magic, that news would have frozen me solid. I thought I was the product of a fated match, but from what this guy is saying, my mother used magic to trick my dad. And if that's the case, how the fuck was I born?

"I remember the deal, Reese," my mother screeches at the fae. "It's not my fault your people couldn't grab him when I left him for you. I thought you guys were good at taking children."

When she left... leaving me alone in the heart of fae territory was her plan?!?

FUCKING BITCH!

The one she called Reese comes over to me and grabs my chin. I can't do anything more than blink at him in response, but my wolf manages a weak growl that rumbles from my chest. The lifting of his black brow is the only indication that he is more observant than the others. The rest of the fae that are mingling around weren't brought for their intelligence apparently as I hear the start of what I think is a flatulence competition.

Reese shakes his head with a chuckle and turns back to my mother.

"Oh, Rebecca," he admonishes. "You forgot that deals with us are binding and if you lie you are forfeit."

She continues to sneer up at the fae, but I can see her hand making movements in the earth next to her, outside of Reese's view. She's working a spell, but unless I can move, I can't counter it. Lifting my chin, I try to angle my head to see what the spell is so I can at least maybe blink a warning in morse code.

Wait a second... I lifted my chin. I try to wiggle my fingers and, although sluggish and weak, they move. Reese glances over to me and gives me a wink. I'm extremely thankful that he did whatever he did, so I'm glad that my mouth is still frozen lest I end up in a fae debt myself.

Digging my fingers into the earth, I send a request out with my magic for the local spirits to lend me their power to stop whatever my mother is building. I don't know if anything is out there at first, but then I feel it. A darkness comes to my call. I don't know what is buried beneath this small city, but waking it is not my intention. I quickly throw up some more walls to prevent it from getting more alert, but I still don't have enough to mess with whatever my mother is trying to pull off.

Reese steps back from my mother as if he can sense what is about to happen. The smile on his face is a reflection of the one my mother had on her own face seconds ago. Now, she shows only confusion. Her magic isn't going to save her this time. I realize too late that I stopped her without meaning to. She was *trying* to wake whatever is buried here, and now she can't...

The fae leader glances at me before returning his focus to my mother.

"We were promised a witch, not a wolf," he leans down to whisper to the woman on the ground in front of him. "Regardless of him being of your blood, he has a wolf. We cannot take wolves from this region due to the bargain struck between our queen and Alpha Elias."

Reese straightens up and the smile on his face is absolutely feral. "You *know* this, Rebecca."

The woman on the ground is no longer anything like the one who I grew up with. Gone is the demanding shrew with the constant verbal attacks. The thing on the ground is openly weeping, begging incoherently for the fae to forgive her and release her from whatever repercussions she must face from her deal. She looks around wildly before setting her sights on me, and her eyes shift in a way I've only noticed once before... the woman has been possessed.

"YOU!" she screams and scrambles toward me. I am not fully mobile or recovered from her magic, so when she climbs on top of me to wrap her hands around my neck, there isn't anything I can do to stop it. It takes all of my concentration to lift my hands to hers, to attempt to pull them off me, but it's no use. My magic is still too weak, so is my body.

My vision starts to fade and I realize this is it... My mother is going to kill me because she can't trade me to the fae to save herself. I'm going to die...

Connor, I love you. I'm sorry.

I hear his growl before the world fades out. At least he heard me... at least he knows he was loved.

On the bright side, at least the wolves won't have to kill me for trespassing.

37

CONNOR

Racing through the underground tunnels, I wonder how in the hell this network exists under the city and no one knows. In response to my thought, I feel the magic pulse from the walls, and there is something further down that I know in my gut we don't want to disturb.

Keep mate away from that, my wolf tells me. As if I didn't already make up my own mind on that one...

Alpha Elias is leading the charge himself to the hill where his warriors have tracked the fae. According to what I've been told, as long as the fae don't harm a wolf or use their magics for anything other than defense, it's not a crime for them to be here. But the fact that they are here at the same time as my mate... it makes me very nervous.

Connor, I love you.

Shaun's voice in my head makes me stumble in my gait. Edward and Elias both glance back at me, but there's no time to figure this out. I can feel him now, and he's dying.

I'm sorry.

I urge another burst of speed out of my wolf to the point the Alpha and vampire are the only ones able to keep up. Elias nudges me to the left and we burst from the mouth of a small cave on the side of a small mountain. I can scent Shaun now, and he's surrounded by fae.

I hear the screeching of a woman, but that doesn't matter to me. I need my mate. I need to save him. I can feel him getting weaker.

I stop as I come to the clearing where they are. The fae are standing around, awaiting orders from the dark haired one who is apparently in charge here. That one is staring down at the woman who is screaming at someone prone on the ground.... That someone is MY MATE.

Before I can do more than growl, Alpha Elias rushes past me in a dark gray blur to rip the woman away from Shaun. The sounds of her pain and fear don't even register to me as I shift back to human. I don't give a shit that I'm naked. I need to help my mate. He's not breathing. His neck and face look like Ethan's did when...

NO! This can't be happening. Shaun doesn't have Ethan's curse. He won't heal from this. He won't come back from the land of the dead like my brother can...

"Shaun, sweetheart, open your eyes," I plead with him as I fall to my knees next to him. There's no response... his heart has stopped. "I can't lose you, baby. Please come back to me."

The tears are falling freely, but I don't care as I put my lips to his and try to force air into him, force life back into him...

Use me, my wolf whispers. *Complete the bond. Save mate.*

Hope lights in my chest. If there's even a miniscule chance this will save him, I have to take it. He tied himself to me to save my life. I must do the same. My world doesn't exist without him in it.

Nuzzling the side of his neck, I whisper, "I'm sorry" before allowing my wolf to take over and lay the claiming bite. The bond between us snaps into place, allowing my wolf to flow into my mate to call forth his own beast. The seconds drag on seemingly forever until his eyes open, a beautiful yellow gaze fading back to chocolate as his wolf fades back to the background. A moment later, he starts coughing and it's the most beautiful sound in the universe.

I gather him up in my arms like I am the only thing tethering him to this plane of existence... maybe I am...

"I need to breathe, Connor," he rasps out, and I flinch even as I resist the urge to hold him tighter. His beautiful voice is destroyed by that bitch.

"It will heal in a few hours," Shaun whispers. "Where is my mother? Did she get away?"

Before I can look up to get him an answer, the fae leader steps up to us. I can't stop the growl as I grip my mate tighter. I *will* protect him, no matter what.

"Easy, Beta," the fae says softly holding his hands up in surrender. "I mean no harm to you or your mate, not now nor any day hence as long as neither of our allegiances change."

Shaun shifts us so that he's sitting in my lap, and I let out a small snort of laughter at the realization that he's covering me so that no one gets a free show. My wolf preens inside me at the thought of our mate being jealous and possessive.

"What's happened, Reese?" Shaun asks, looking to the fae. I'm guessing they had a chance to talk a bit before the woman attacked... his own mother. I mean, I know my mother did those things to Ethan, but even in her most crazed state, she never even raised her voice to me. How does a woman do this kind of thing to her own flesh and blood?

The fae looks around the clearing, making sure the rest of his kind have dispersed, before speaking.

"Rebecca has created a situation I can't make a decision on," he tells us. "She is forsworn and belongs to the fae, bound doubly through both her debt and her attempt to subvert and lie. But then she attempted to kill you, her kin, who is under the protection of many powerful beings. Those powers will want their vengeance and retribution. I cannot take her back to Faerie until those beings release their claims."

Glancing down at my mate, his confusion is written on his face. He hasn't seen Alpha Elias in human form yet. I doubt he's even glanced at any of the wolves in the clearing.

"Not attempted," he whispers. "She did kill me. I was dead."

Multiple growls echo through the frigid night, and my mate

shivers in my arms. I'm completely naked, but until this moment, I hadn't noticed the cold. It won't do any lasting damage to me, but I want my mate warm and safe.

"Alpha?" I call out. "King Edward? Can we get someone to take us back to the house? We're not exactly dressed for the weather, and I'd like to get my mate checked out by a doctor as soon as possible."

At my request, the vampire strides over to us. I fight back my wolf when he grips my mate's chin to look into his eyes. Shaun doesn't fight it. He looks resigned and exhausted.

"I'll drive you both back," he says after what I can only assume was a mental conversation with the Alpha. "We can take the SUV that Rebecca drove here."

Shaun is practically dead weight as I lift him from the ground to carry him to the vehicle; however, when Reese opens the back door for us, my mate starts clawing at me to get away. There's a high pitched whining coming from his throat that breaks my heart. I've only ever heard that noise from Ethan, and it usually precedes a panic attack.

I quickly turn away from the SUV and wait for the sound of the door closing before I turn back around. His shivering has intensified, and I don't know if it is from the cold or if it is caused by the trauma. All I want is to get him somewhere safe and warm.

"Not..." he starts, but the tremors wracking his body make it difficult to understand. "Not... seat... spell..."

I just lean against a tree and hold him to me, hoping he can calm down enough to be more clear. But it's becoming obvious that it isn't going to happen. I really don't want to have to carry him through those tunnels while naked, but it looks like it's the only option at this point.

"He was brought in the backseat," the fae man, Reese says from my left. I jump at his sudden appearance. He was at the car not a second ago. "Rebecca had used a spell to restrain him, but I hadn't realized the spell was within the confines of the vehicle itself. I'm not a witch to be able to sense such things, so I cannot say if it still exists."

Looking down at Shaun, he nods an affirmation to the fae's assumption of the problem. Well that's easy to fix.

"If it's a matter of a problem with the backseat, you'll just have to sit on my lap in the front," I tell him, nuzzling the fresh bite mark on his neck. His exasperated giggle is the most wonderful sound I have ever heard.

38

SHAUN

I try not to fall asleep on the way to the Alpha house. There is nowhere more comfortable than Connor's arms for me right now. I know a big part of that is the claiming bite he put on me, but I'm too exhausted to worry about that right now. I know I'm dreaming while my body is safe and secure in the arms of my mate, but it's still a strange occurrence to be in woods that I know don't exist in our reality.

"So you finally decide to visit me, Mr. Cleary?" a strange little punk girl asks as she appears directly in front of me. "I don't like to be kept waiting. It doesn't happen all that often."

Taking in her appearance and from what Ethan has shared with me, I'm pretty sure I know who this is and why I'm here. I try to pull myself away from the dream, but there's something blocking my magic...That's a first for my dreams...

"Yes, I'm the infamous Cassie," she says, jumping up on a boulder that wasn't there before. "And as for your magic, it's still waking up from that bitch's interference."

Picking a daisy from next to her, she starts pulling the petals off like she's trying to make a decision. I'm beginning to understand why Ric and Ethan were so frustrated by her.

"Thank you, by the way. I didn't have a plan in place to reseal the creature under the city, and she was dangerously close to letting it out. The little bit of magic you pushed into the earth was enough to strengthen the seal beyond her reach."

When I stay silent, she jumps down from her perch to stand in front of me... almost an entire foot shorter than me. Glancing down at her, she smiles shyly at me.

"You're not as direct as the others," she says, twisting a strand of her neon pink hair around her finger. "You won't fight or question what I have planned for you, will you?"

I shake my head because there's no point in fighting against one of the fates when they're right in front of you. I may have a touch of clairvoyance, at least enough to get feelings about things, but I'm not one to assume I know or understand the fates or what they see. Plus, I have seen the episode of Supernatural enough times to know you don't go off all Team Free Will on the fates, not that I'm going to ever want to un-sink the Titanic or anything...

She tilts her head like a dog before standing on her tiptoes to pull me down by the tie I'm disgusted to still be wearing. Leaning in to whisper, she asks, "And what if I plan to take Connor away from you forever?"

On instinct alone, I throw the small woman away from me. I expect my wolf to come to the forefront, but he is conspicuously absent. I feel my expression morph from rage to shock and fear.

I just threw one of the fates around like a ragdoll. My wolf isn't with me. My magic is still trapped.

Fuck me, I'm a dead man.

While I contemplate dying for the second time in as many hours, the little punk starts rolling on the ground in laughter.

"Oh, I *like* you," she finally manages to gasp out between guffaws. "Relax, werewitch. Your man is your own and the two of you will raise two wonderful sons, although the witch is going to be problematic for a while."

My jaw drops in shock. Sons?

"Neither of us is omega," I tell her and she just nods her head like I said something stupid and she's waiting for me to think it through.

Standing up, she brushes the dirt off of her clothing before grabbing my hand. "But you are magic. Where there's a need, fate finds a way," she tells me before popping out of sight.

What the fuck does that mean?

I jolt awake in a strange bed. The only thing keeping the panic clawing up my throat from taking over is being surrounded by the scent of fries and funnel cakes... Connor is here. My mate is here. Fate hasn't taken him from me after all.

39

CONNOR

I sense the moment Shaun first wakes up. His panic almost has me running back to the guest room that Alpha Elias has set us up in, but I feel him settle almost immediately back into a light sleep. The last twenty four hours have ranked up there with the worst moments of my entire life.

Thinking I lost Ethan almost a decade ago was torture, but I survived. I would not survive it if I had lost Shaun last night. I can't stop the shiver that runs up my spine at the memory of holding his lifeless body.

"You alright, son?"

The Alpha's voice cuts into my memories bringing me back to the task at hand... figuring out what to do with Diane Cleary, whose real name is apparently Rebecca.

"Is Shaun's last name really Cleary?" I ask before I can stop the question from coming out. I got *some* sleep when we got back to the house, but it was far from restful. My brain still isn't firing on all cylinders yet.

There's a chuckle that flows through the room of warriors and high-ranking wolves at my question. It was decided that after lunch, we would have this planning session, but we haven't really started anything deep yet. The Alpha decreed that his grandson is to be a part of everything, so the room is just mingling right now. This is the part I always hated with the events my parents hosted... pointless small talk and posturing.

"Cleary was David's mother's family name," says an older wolf from my right. "She was the Beta's only daughter and it was voted that she should be the Alpha Mate but the woman downright refused a mating mark."

"Had me convinced for years that David wasn't my son," Elias chuckles before taking a sip of his tea. "It wasn't until the boy shifted into his wolf that anyone saw a resemblance. By that time, he decided he was going to be my Beta and there was nothing anyone could do about it."

The picture I only guessed at before is getting clearer the more the older wolves reminisce about the past, but I don't want any other tidbits of my mate's life to be revealed without him in the room, so I attempt to change the subject.

"Where exactly am I now?" I ask before they can get deeper into their memories. "King Edward just kind of rushed me over, so I didn't have a chance to take note of the journey."

The vampire in question glances up from his phone at the mention of his name, but then goes back to whatever was holding his interest. I'm not sure what that is about, but I can feel a tingle of unease that the vampire is so focused on the electronic device.

Alpha Elias nods to me before setting down his mug of tea and sitting up straighter.

"I guess we should get started sooner rather than later," he says under his breath before looking around the room. "Everyone is here that needs to be except my grandson, but we can let him sleep a little more and get the formalities out of the way."

"I assume you mean me," says a soft voice from the doorway. I didn't know he had even woken back up, so I rush over to him, scouring him for further injuries. Before I get carried away, he grabs my hand to place it on his cheek.

"I'm fine," he tells me. His voice still not fully recovered, yet sounding a million times better. "Let's sit and listen to the man who claims to be my grandfather."

And then later, we are going to pick up where we left off in that motel room.

The sound of a mug shattering from across the room lets me know that I wasn't the only one who heard my mate's thoughts. I whip my head around to glare daggers at the vampire. He at least has the decency to look apologetic...

I apologize for overhearing, he sends to us, raising his hands in surrender. *I was unprepared for anyone being able to use this ability outside of my own bloodline.*

Glancing back at Shaun, he looks embarrassed but mouths the word "later" to me. Nodding my understanding, I pick him up and carry him over to my seat, placing him on my lap for the discussion, much to the surprise and delight of everyone in the room. There doesn't seem to be a single wolf of this powerful pack that has an issue with a beta and alpha being mated, even both being men.

"We may be old, but we are very progressive as far as packs go," the ancient she-wolf in the corner pipes up in response to the confusion I'm sure is showing on my face. "My boys know better than to be bigots. I'm not too old to put them over my knee."

A round of laughter flows through the room, and all of the tension seems to fall away. Before the Alpha can get things back on track, Shaun leans more heavily into my chest but directs a question to the she-wolf. "Are you truly the matriarch? Or just an honorary mother to the wolves here?"

Alpha Elias picks up his mug to hide his smile, but nods to the woman that she can answer. It seems the action is merely a formality for the sake of being in mixed company based on the snort she directs back at him and the chuckles that follow around the room.

"Young man, you are my great-great-grandson on your father's side," she says conspiratorially, leaning toward us. "I birthed a total of seventeen pups, and most of the men in this room are related to me in some way. Makes is difficult for our pack to find mates, what with everyone being my grandchildren and all."

The sounds of sputtering and coughing fill the room at the sheer lack of tact shown by this woman, but my mate can't contain his laughter. I feel the smile break out on my face at the complete lack of restraint for his joy. I would give anything to see him like this always.

40

SHAUN

The old bat is hilarious! I love her. Regardless of whether or not it's truth that she is my blood relation, I'm claiming her.

"Nana, I love you," I gasp out between the laughter. I don't notice right away that the room goes silent, but Connor's arms tightening around my waist make me realize I might have said something wrong.

"Not wrong, Son," says the older wolf to our right. "It's just that the only one who ever called her Nana was your father, David."

I look to the old woman and notice tears in her eyes, but her toothless smile has me smiling back. It's kind of creepy, but oddly comforting at the same time.

The Alpha clears his throat to get all of our attention. He flashes a brief smile my way before addressing the room.

"Rebecca has created an unsolvable problem with her latest scheme. Had she not harmed her son, the fae would have first claim to her blood."

I glance up at Connor to see if he's just as confused as I am, but it looks like he has a few more answers than I do. The fae should have her dead to rights for the broken deal. They even can go after her for kin-slaying based on their laws, but I'm not seeing how any of this negates their claim.

"Um," I interrupt. "Not trying to be rude or disrespectful, Alpha, but how is this unsolvable? By fae law, as dictated by the true Queen in the age before the merging of the realms, a deal made or fulfilled by deceit makes the forsworn life forfeit to the fae for punishment. Furthermore, to commit the act of kin-slaying in front of one of the nobles of Faerie without just cause according to fae law also results in forfeiture of life to the fae."

Looking around the room, I see a lot of heads nodding, but Reese lowers his head before directing his attention to the Alpha.

"I'm not your Alpha. I'm your grandfather," the older man gently admonishes me. "Call me Elias, Pops, Gramps, whatever... just not Alpha. I'm not that for you.

"As to the other things you've stated, those are all true by *fae* law. And don't think I'm going to overlook why you know fae law to this degree. You are a wolf and a witch. There's a story behind that which I expect to hear at some point, but that's for later," he wags his finger at me like I'm a pup behaving badly. I feel the chuckle from beneath me and don't fight the smile that pulls at my lips.

"The issue arises that fae law has no bearing inside my pack when a wolf is harmed by an outsider. Regardless of said wolf's affiliation with the pack, it is written into the very land by ancient magics... a fact your mother was well aware of considering she was banished for having already broken it once before."

It takes me a second to realize what he's referring to, but a glance at Reese tells me the train of thought I'm on is the right one. My mother stole the Alpha Heir and Beta away using magic and harmed another wolf in the process.

"So why isn't Reese banished?" I ask. "He helped my mother back then, right?"

A low growl vibrates through the room, making the fae look nervous for the first time since I met him. Granted it's been less than a day, but it is enough to make me realize I shouldn't have asked such a question.

The Alpha, Elias, stands up and the room goes silent once more.

"Reese had no idea the spell Rebecca was planning to use was going to do anything more than cloud David's judgment," he snarls to the room and each wolf's head, except Nana's and our own, tilts to show subservience. "To the fae, fated mates are a mythical thing that no longer exists. He had no way of knowing that the spell Rebecca planned to use was one to overtake a mate bond. He didn't know the spell would kill Sheila."

A wolf in the far corner surges to his feet in anger, "My daughter is dead because that THING gave that BITCH the power needed to kill my little girl! She should have been Alpha Mate and instead she is in the ground!"

A few wolves around him try to get him to settle while others grumble their agreement. Those in agreement seem to be glaring at me like I'm the embodiment of everything bad in the world. Connor's growl in response to their stares seems to set the grieving father off again. Only this time, his anger is directed at me.

"And now we have a fucking abomination in our midst!" he shouts while pointing at me. "The fruit of evil can only be evil itself! *You* killed my Sheila by being born!"

Chaos is erupting in the room and there is nothing I can do about it. I didn't have a choice in being born. I didn't have a choice in who my mother is...

I try to remove the steel bands of Connor's arms so that I can flee the room. I don't belong here. I'm the living proof of the disgusting excuse of a human that my mother is. They don't need to see me. They need to deal with her. I'll just disappear and...

"You will do NO such thing," Connor growls in my ear, forcing me to ignore the sounds of fighting in the room beyond our personal bubble. "You are mine and I am yours. Where you go, I go. And I'm done running from the secrets. If nothing else, we are getting all of the answers before we go home... home to Ethan and the triplets. *They* are our family. If you want to leave this behind, we will. But not before we get all the answers."

He gentles his tone before saying, "*You* are worth it. *You* deserve answers."

I stop fighting to get free and instead fight to pull him closer. I need this man. I love this man. They can pry him from my cold dead hands...

41

CONNOR

"ENOUGH!" a woman's voice rings out, while a concussive blast knocks everyone standing on their asses, including the Alpha.

The cackling laughter of the old she-wolf Shaun called Nana can be heard in the silence that follows.

"Eliza, dear, so good of you to respond to my invitation," the she-wolf says to the elegant woman who seems to have appeared out of nowhere in the center of the room.

"Cynthia, you should have told me sooner that my wayward daughter was caught," the woman replies to the she-wolf, ignoring the groans from all of the men scattered across the floor. "And what is this news that I have a grandson? Why is this the first I'm hearing about this?"

The elegant witch turns to face us, and I watch as her expression melts from haughty and cold to the genuine affection you would expect from a grandmother. It only takes two steps for Eliza to reach us, and I can feel Shaun's grip tighten on my wrist to the point of being painful. It takes me by surprise, but after completing our bond, I know exactly how he feels about this woman, so I place a light kiss on the back of his neck in support.

"You have my husband's eyes," she whispers to him, gently cupping his cheek. I can feel her magic pulse through both of us, but it is a comforting warmth compared to other magics I've felt. "How could boys as pure as you both come from such monsters?"

We both tense at her words. How much did she see?

Before I can question her, she turns to the men on the floor to ask, "Why are you all squabbling instead of figuring out who has the lawful right to kill my bitch of a daughter, Elias?"

Nana is back to cackling and the wolves who had remained seated all let out a sigh of relief that we are getting back on track. The Alpha offers his chair to the witch with the sweep of his arm, and he comes next to the chair my mate and I are sharing in to address the room again.

"Thank you for the assistance, as always, Eliza," he grits out while rubbing the heel of his hand into his left butt cheek. "And you are correct. The issue isn't whether or not Rebecca will die, but by whose hand."

42

SHAUN

I'm still reeling mentally and emotionally from discovering I have grandparents. Not only do I have grandparents, but they actually seem to give a shit about me. I didn't even realize that my dad was the only one of my parents who cared until the day my mother found my secret stash of lace. Yeah, she flipped out on me every time we had to move because of me, but I thought for some reason she was afraid my magic tipped off some bounty hunters or something.

I thought she was afraid *for me...*

The knowledge that my mother only had me as an insurance policy cuts deeper than I want to admit. A part of me had selfishly held out the hope that she loved me in her own way... her hands around my throat kind of disavowed me of that notion.

The arms around me give me a little squeeze, bringing me back to the discussion raging around us. "You alright, my love?" Connor whispers, placing a kiss to my shoulder. "Do you need a minute away from all of this? It can't be easy hearing how much everyone wants to kill your mother."

I laugh in response to his statement and every head in the room turns to us. The snort turns into full blown belly laughter at the absurdity of the situation. My mate and I should hold a fucking contest to figure out which mother was worse. Hell, even *I* don't know who would win that contest. All I know is we both lost, although Ethan got it the worst...

Thoughts of what my best friend went through makes me stiffen in Connor's arms, and I know I have to get it all off my chest and get the answers I need. One thing is for certain, though. No one in this room has a better claim to kill the bitch than me. *I'm* the one she actually killed... not a relative, not a fucking broken deal. *She killed me* and a life debt trumps all.

"I think it's time to just end this," I announce to the room before Sheila's father can start up again about how he needs to avenge his daughter. "No one has a better claim on her life than I do, but I won't be the one to take her life."

The old ass jumps up to argue, but Eliza makes a hand gesture that sends him flying back into his seat. I need to learn that trick...

"My grandson was speaking, Pup," she snarls at the wolf before throwing a wink my way. He looks to be at least twenty years her senior, but if she's calling him pup... She mouths the word 'later' to me and I turn back to the room in general to continue.

"Just because I won't kill her myself doesn't mean I will stand in the way of the one who does the deed. We need answers before she pays the price she earned, so I formally request the right to question my killer."

The room is silent until Nana speaks up.

"First time I've ever heard of a murder victim confronting their killer, but it's within his rights as a victim to confront his attacker per the pack law," she mutters almost to herself, but it's loud enough that we all hear it. To the room in general she growls, "None of you pups better have a problem with it or else you will face me."

She sends me a reassuring smile, and I can't help the one I show back to her.

"Grandma is correct," Elias says from next to our chair. "Shaun has the right to question her before any of us take action. Let's have some dinner and get some rest. We will witness the interrogation in the morning in the catacombs."

Leaning down, he asks "Unless you want it to be private? You have that right."

I look around the room before answering him. "I don't care who hears what she says to me as long as they can be silent and not interrupt. I need answers to questions I didn't dare think to ask when I thought there was a chance..."

My voice breaks and I can't bring myself to say the words out loud. Connor seems to understand and finishes my thought for me.

"There are things you can't admit you need to know until you accept that the person who is supposed to love you isn't the hero but really a monster in disguise."

43

CONNOR

Shaun and I bypass the group dinner and just carry some food up to the room. We eat in silence, but I can feel his need to talk. I'm patient. I'll wait him out if I have to, but I can't hold back my curiosity as to what he wants to talk about. Now that I can feel his emotions, I'm not worried that he doesn't want me. I can feel his need. It's the same as my own.

"I know you want to talk, but can I say something first?" I ask him as he sets his plate on the chair by the door. He nods as he sits down next to me on the bed. This is going to be very awkward considering he doesn't know I overheard him all those months ago. It's time I come clean about that, so that we don't have any more misunderstandings like we did at the motel.

"I heard you when you told your friend you were a virgin," I blurt out before I can lose my nerve. "I heard you and I heard about the panties and I haven't had a day since then that my dick hasn't been hard thinking about what I heard."

The silence next to me is making me nervous. I feel a wall slam inside my head and suddenly I can't feel Shaun's emotions either. I hurriedly turn to him and grab his hands before he can run. They are like ice. I summon all of my courage and lift my gaze to his face. I didn't know it was possible to blush and pale at the same time, but somehow my mate has managed it.

After reassuring myself that he is neither choking, nor in any real danger of spontaneous combustion, I opt to continue, to hopefully get us past this hurdle in our relationship and fully seal our bond.

"I can only assume that the other day in the motel room you had your freak out over me seeing your pretty lace." His squeak and jerk of the head gives me the courage I need to continue on. I'm not sure it's an affirmation, but I hope so. "And let me tell you, you are gorgeous in that jock and I hope you have many many more pieces to show me. That was the hottest thing I have ever experienced... well, up until the part where you freaked out and ran away to get kidnapped by the wicked bitch of the wempghpf..."

Shaun cuts off my words by practically tackling me and planting a kiss on me. I can do nothing else but open myself to him and let him do whatever he damn well pleases. This has always been and will always be his show.

Pulling back to take a breath, he makes the demand, "Give me control. I can't submit. I can't be what I'm not. I'm not submissive." Each sentence is punctuated with a kiss to a different part of my body. My shirt has made its way to the other end of the room somehow without me lifting my arms, but I don't care. My mate is here and touching me and loving me. This is all I want.

"It's yours," I whisper to the ceiling as I hear the zipper on my jeans going down. "Everything I am, it's yours to use as you wish. Command me, my love."

I feel the tug as my pants are pulled down my legs followed by a gasp of surprise. I hurry to look down my body to see Shaun staring at my naked crotch. Before I can really guess what the issue is, he smirks and takes me in his mouth and all thought leaves my head. It's a struggle to keep my hands to myself, but I can tell he needs to do this on his own. My mate will get everything and anything he wants with me. Now and forever... if only I can keep myself from coming long enough for him to get his pleasure as well.

44

SHAUN

I feel like I'm on fire. Is this what omegas feel when they are in heat? No, Ethan says it's impossible to resist any type of sex when he's in heat, even if it's with a total stranger. If this is only a fraction of what he has to experience, I have a newfound respect for Ethan and Ric being able to walk after those few days of heat sex. This is unbearable. I need to have all of my mate. I need to be inside of him, have him inside of me.

I still can't feel my magic, but somehow it answers my call and rips his shirt away so that I can continue my lips' explorations down his body. Where my skin is riddled with scars from when I was left to fend for myself as a teenager, his is perfection. I work my way down to his pants and it's like déjà vu in the best possible way, repeating the process of removing his jeans, just like in the motel.

As I yank them down, I freeze for a second. He isn't wearing underwear... He had them in the motel, so where did they go? I look up to meet his gaze and he seems genuinely concerned that I stopped. Then it hits me where his underwear went. It's still in the motel room in Pennsylvania. I paid up for a few days, so they're probably still hanging off the lamp where they landed last time. The place didn't exactly scream maid service...

"Before I start, I have to know..."

"Only once, and with a human," Connor whimpers as I run my fingers lightly along his length. "He had on a lace teddy and... hrghrhghr..."

His words cut off as I take Connor in my mouth, but I don't make the same mistake as last time. Instead of taking all of him at once, I focus on the tip, pushing my tongue under his foreskin, tasting the essence of my mate. His scent is still heavenly, but there's a deeper musk that is driving my arousal higher. Combined with the noises he's making, there's no doubt in my mind that we are truly meant to be.

After a few minutes of bringing him to the brink of coming, I force myself to back off and sit up. I look down at my conquest and can't help but feel powerful in that moment. This man wants me, but *I* get to choose what and how much he receives. It's a heady feeling, and one that I don't take lightly.

"Please let me taste you," he begs, clenching his fists at his sides. I want to test his obedience.

No... I *need* to test his obedience.

"Hands behind your back," I tell him and he immediately complies. "Good boy."

If I hadn't been watching his face, I might have missed it, but Connor couldn't hide the split second of surprise followed by the rapture he felt at those words. That look makes me want to always be the reason behind his pleasure.

Mate is ours. No one else's, my wolf snarls in my head. His moment of possessiveness makes me realize I share it. Connor is MINE.

Slowly, I slide up his body, bringing both hands to circle his neck. Leaning forward, I lick along the edge of his ear, relishing in the shiver that goes through him.

"I want to tag you, collar you, brand you as mine," I whisper in his ear.

I can feel the pre-cum dripping from his cock as it soaks the slacks I'm still wearing. That bit of moisture reminds me that I'm still in the clothing that my mother put me in and it's enough to start my pulse rising again, and not in a good way. I bury my face into

Connor's neck and inhale, hoping that his scent will be enough to stave off the panic so that we can finally have this moment.

"Can I touch you, my love?" he begs softly. He hasn't moved his arms from behind him, but I can feel the tension in his shoulders. He wants to move, but he's desperate to prove to me that I can trust him to listen. The clear submission is enough to shatter the last wall around my heart.

Choking back a sob, I manage to get out one command. It might not be the declaration of undying love that these feelings call for, but it's the only thing that makes sense to me in this scenario...

"Take these clothes off of me and get on all fours."

I need this man more than I need my next breath, but what I really need is for him to help me remove the last piece of my mother's control. I can't do it alone, and Connor is the only one I can trust to not hurt me. Despite everything we've been through, everything he's done and I've run from, in my heart and soul, I know he would never do anything to bring me to harm.

45

CONNOR

There is fear in both his eyes and his voice when he gives me the command to undress him, so I do the only thing I can.

I obey.

Pulling my hands from behind my back, I use them to push Shaun into a sitting position above me. I haven't done sit-ups since high school, but being a werewolf has its perks. I pull my upper body upright and begin the slow process of releasing each button on the horrible shirt he's wearing. My mate should only be dressed for comfort or luxury, not this overly starched poly blend monstrosity.

"You're too slow, boy," Shaun growls out, leaning back further to give me better access. "You have ten seconds to get me naked or you don't get to come tonight. I'll stuff your hole and leave you wanting."

Buttons go flying in all directions and I'm pretty sure I hear glass breaking, but my mate is gloriously naked in under eight seconds following his statement. I have to swallow hard lest I start drooling at the sight in front of me. Tracing my fingertips over the scars made by my own claws, I wonder for the millionth time how am I so blessed after everything I've done?

"Did you forget your orders, boy?"

I look up at the face of my mate and see only joy and passion reflected in his eyes. He gives my hip a gentle tap and I smile before rolling over to my stomach. Shaun lifts himself up onto his knees enough for me to be able to bring my legs forward and get up on all fours like he ordered me to. The anticipation is killing me.

This is nothing like that night at the frat house. I feel like I won't be able to take another full breath until my mate is inside of me, owning me...breeding me.

I feel his strong fingers grip my hips and the only thing I can imagine is his dick entering me, so it comes as a shock to feel his tongue slide from my balls up to meet the pucker of my asshole. It isn't exactly a bad sensation, but certainly unexpected. I jolt forward slightly at the feel of his tongue pushing into me, but the growl he releases allows me to settle and relax back into his ministrations. My mate is obviously a natural talent, and I'll do anything to keep this going...

I don't know how long he spends softening me up, but I'm nothing but pure need by the time he sits back and reaches for the side table to grab something. I didn't even notice before, but someone put a bottle of lube in the room for us. Huh, that's a weird thing to put in a guestroom.

We aren't omega, my wolf chuckles. I have to bite my lip to keep my embarrassment in check. Logically I know that my body wouldn't produce slick, but I am so desperate to have my mate take me in every way possible that I apparently forgot.

Before I can beg for the return of his touch, Shaun pushes what feels like two fingers inside me. I can feel my need only growing stronger as a rumbling noise starts in my chest. When he adds a third, the sound gets louder and I can finally recognize what it reminds me of...

"Are you fucking purring?" my mate asks, pulling his fingers out of my ass, leaning down to cover my body with his own. "That's hot."

Did my mate just do a fucking Paris Hilton impression after fingering my ass for twenty minutes?!

My head barely starts to turn and look at him when I feel the head of his cock pushing into me. It burns just like I remember from horrible previous escapade, but at the same time, this is an entirely new experience. I realize in this moment that it is true what they say, the person you're with makes all the difference. Shaun is the only man I ever want to do this with, and thankfully fate has seen fit to ensure it.

"Please, Master," I whimper when he stills behind me after bottoming out. I can feel the satisfaction through our bond and know that he will want that title in the bedroom from now on. I have zero issues giving him that, especially considering the way he starts pounding me into the fucking mattress like a man possessed. I am definitely going to want this every single night...

We are both a sweaty grunting mess by the time Shaun's rhythm starts to falter. Words failed me long ago. Every breath is a gasping struggle not to come, but I won't without my Master's permission.

"Let go, boy," he growls out before pushing deeper than he's gone before and stills. "Come for me."

As I feel his release pumping inside of me, I finally let go with a scream. My mate has marked me inside and out. No one else will ever have me... My vision starts to turn grey around the edges. I've never orgasmed so hard in my life...

Somehow, Shaun manages to tilt us to the side enough that I don't collapse into my mess and I let exhaustion carry me into dreamland.

46

SHAUN

For a first time, that was one hell of an experience. I was so concerned about being a two pump chump, that looking down on my sleeping mate, I'm afraid I might have over corrected. What I wanted to be a tender loving moment turned into a power exchange the likes I never could have imagined.

In what world does an alpha wolf submit to anyone other than their Alpha? It just doesn't happen... And yet it did. For me, Connor submitted completely.

Pulling my now soft dick out of him, I marvel at the sight of my release escaping before his hole closes itself back up. Now, *that* is a sight I want to happen regularly...

A phone ringing from the other end of the room has me sitting up straighter. I know it's not mine. I have no clue what my mother did with my phone when she changed my clothes. Looking around for the source of the ringing, I can't stop the smile when I see the scraps of cloth that used to be the clothing I was wearing.

My mate did a wonderful job of taking care of me.

The ringing stops and pulls my attention back to the present. The room is a wreck. There's a pile of broken glass by the door. Looking closer, it appears that one of the buttons shattered a drinking glass from our dinner. I don't want anyone to worry about cleaning up after us, so I take advantage of my mate sleeping off our activities to crawl out of bed. The least I can do is pick up what I can. Slipping on Connor's shirt, I find myself wishing I at least had some of my underwear. Even with his shirt, I still feel tainted by my mother's hands on me. I need my pretties to feel like myself again.

"Would this help?"

I'm rather ashamed of the sound that comes out of my mouth. As a grown man, such a sound should not be possible...

I try to slow the racing heartbeat caused by Cassie suddenly appearing in front of me. She shoves my backpack into my hands when I apparently can do nothing more than stare. In my defense, who the hell is ever prepared for one of the fates to pop in unannounced at two fifty seven in the morning?

"Your bestie is the one who sent me, so you know," she says plainly, brushing scraps of fabric off the loveseat in the corner. "He got worried when your mate didn't answer the phone."

"The phone literally just stopped ringing thirty seconds ago," I tell her, digging into the main compartment of my bag in search of one of my full coverage panties. I may want pretty and I might not be into women, but I'll be damned if I'm giving her a free show.

I slip into the attached bath once I've chosen a pair. Wetting a washcloth with warm water, I clean myself up and proceed to pull on my black satin bikini cut panties. With the softness on my skin, I let out the last of my tension. Finally feeling like myself again, I wet another rag to clean up my mate, who is a surprisingly heavy sleeper considering the amount of noise the fate has made since showing up.

"Oh, Ethan was going to fret and worry and keep *his* mate awake which would keep the babies up which would cause Jack to miss out on sleep and then fail a test and create all kinds of havoc before I'd have to step in to make corrections," she mutters as I come back into the room. "I just figured this was easier for everyone if I showed up to set his mind at ease."

She flips a phone around to show me the messages screen... It's Connor's phone and she used it to send a picture of my mate's naked ass to his baby brother... Holy Fuck, he's gonna shit a brick over this...

With a smile cracking on my face, the only thought in my head is *I can't wait to see it.*

"Can't wait to see what?" Connor asks as he rolls over with a groan. As his ass comes into contact with the wet spot on the bed, he yelps and jumps out of the bed. Cassie lets out a giggle and my own laughter turns to a growl as I rush to block my naked mate from her view.

"Relax, Werewitch. I've seen the show many times," she tells me, tossing the phone to my overly perplexed mate. "My job for the night is done. Just remember, the bitch of east met the bitch of the west and their boys are single no more."

With those cryptic words, she pops back into the ether like she was never there.

"Love?" Connor asks, pulling me back against him.

"Hmm?"

"Who the fuck was that?"

I giggle and turn to plant a light kiss on his lips before responding, "That, my boy, was fate."

47

CONNOR

My ass hurts...

The choking sound from the other end of the room reminds me that I'm in the presence of someone who can read thoughts. I duck out of Edward's line of sight and try to stop the blush I'm sure is in full bloom on my cheeks. I'm horribly out of practice for schooling my thoughts since I spent most of the last year avoiding everyone.

I finally manage to locate Shaun in the amphitheater-style cavern talking to his grandmother. As I make my way over, our eyes meet and I flash back to this morning before breakfast. After a wonderful experimentation with the sixty-nine position, my Master gave me a choice. I could choose his pretty for the day and go commando myself, or I could elect to be in the dark and get one spank later for each time he catches me looking until I can guess.

Never thought I would rack up twenty seven glances over the course of one meal...

"Connor Sinclair!" Edward shouts from across the room, and my mate's eyebrows raise in question. I run behind him quickly, much to the amusement of almost every elder in the room.

"If you cannot school your thoughts, please have your mate assist you in constructing a mental barrier," the vampire says when he reaches us. "I do NOT need to be hearing about my step-grandson's sex-capades."

A round of laughter echoes in the room before a shrill whistle brings everyone's attention to Alpha Elias.

"If you will all take your seats, it's time to get this shindig started," he says as he nods to a guard on the other end of the room. "My grandson, Shaun, has first right to question the condemned, but once he's finished, I will be the one to determine the order of interrogations if anyone else wants answers before she is executed."

Shaun sits to the left of the Alpha, and I take my space next to him. Earlier, I told him I wanted to show that he is the one in charge, that I'm not alpha when he's with me, but he insists that outside of our pack and family that we need to show we are equals. I know we are equals, but he seems to think that others will not understand and take offense on my behalf. I say to let them be offended because I'm not.

I'm not ashamed that this man is my Master, my love, my everything. Alpha, beta, or omega... it doesn't matter. He completes me and lets me just *be me* in a way that I haven't felt since I was a child. Having someone to please and care for completes me. Having someone care enough to notice what I'm doing and actually call me on my shit when I get off course... *that* is what my Master gives me. He leads and I will follow.

My eyes are pulled away from Shaun by the screeching of a banshee from the center of the room. Correction, that banshee is my de-facto mother-in-law, and from what I can make out, she seems to think that someone will come to her rescue here.

Oh my sweet boy, she has no idea half of what her body managed to do lately.

My body tenses at that whispered voice. Shaun feels the change in me, and looks at me with concern. Licking my lips, I try to figure out how to tell him that my mother is also to blame. I can feel her trying to gain entry to my body again, and the terror induced by even the thought of that has my mate standing in front of me, gripping my face in both his hands.

"What is it, baby?" he asks me, searching my face for what has me so spooked.

I try to open my mouth to speak, but nothing happens... *This can't be happening again!*

Edward is suddenly next to us with a hand on each of our shoulders, and I feel like I can breathe a little easier.

Easy, Connor, the vampire breathes into my mind. *She cannot take over the way she did before, but your fear is giving her enough control to stop your speech.*

"FUCK THAT BITCH!" Shaun growls with enough force to cause everyone but the most senior beings in the room to fall to their knees. Gripping my chin, he wrenches my head to the side before uttering to me, "You are *MINE* and that bitch needs to get it through her undead fucking head that I do NOT share what is mine!"

The feeling of his canines piercing my skin is enough to send the shadow of my mother outside of my body, but the flow of magic and feeling of possession settles into me a sense of rightness that was previously missing, even after all of our reconciliations the last few days. I hadn't realized it, but before this moment, we were both still holding back. I feel my wolf sending everything that we are back through the bond. *THIS* is what a true mate bond is supposed to be.

*Dirty fucking mongrel...*my mother's voice echoes in the chamber. She's stopped speaking to just me. Apparently, she got enough power somehow to speak to us all, and it is obvious that no one in the room is a fan of a disembodied voice calling out a slur. The growls steadily grow until the Alpha puts a stop to it.

"SILENCE!" Elias roars out before glancing to his left. "Who are you, intruder, to speak in this chamber?"

Shaun meets his grandfather's eyes before pulling me into his chest. "I'm so sorry, baby."

Wait... Sorry?

48

SHAUN

I fucked up. By completing the bond with Connor just now, I gave Esther the fucking power boost she needed to exist outside of a host. I had my suspicions that Mrs. Sinclair was the one behind my mother's irrational behavior after realizing she was possessed, but this is getting fucking ridiculous. How far is this dead bitch going to go to try and stop her son from being with me?

Letting go of my mate, I stand in front of him to add another barrier between him and the undead witch. The wolves in the room can't see her. The other witches in the room can't see her. I don't even know if King Edward can see her, but I can. When the bond completed, our magics mingled. Connor's latent witchblood abilities flowed into me, and now I have their family's abilities with the dead.

"Esther, you have no rights here," I say to her, making sure she notices that I can see her. "You will answer our questions or you will leave. Either way, you *will* keep your filthy claws off of my mate."

The psychic blast sent through the room in response to my declaration has many of the wolves grimacing or gripping their heads in pain, but I laugh. That was nothing compared to the pain Ethan was blasting out during his contractions. Hell, it was nothing compared to Ethan when he thought his brother wasn't going to go to his birthday...

That reminds me…

I throw my magic at the spirit of Esther Sinclair and feel it bind her to my will. My rage at how she treated her son after her death is NOTHING to what I feel toward how the woman treated my best friend. The woman thought nothing of beating, imprisoning, and literally vivisecting a fucking child, from the time he was four years old through his thirteenth birthday.

A part of me always thought it was a bit unfair that she didn't suffer more for all the pain she caused.

"I thought so, too."

The voice next to me makes me jump, but only because I know my grandfather was to my right and he definitely doesn't sound like a teenage girl…

Elias has fallen back on his ass in apparent surprise from having a tiny punk girl pop up in front of him from the ether. The look on his face is enough to crack through the rage, and I can't stop the snort of laughter that escapes. It's pointless to hold it in, and I double over, trying to catch my breath.

"Glad to know I'm amusing," the Alpha rumbles good-naturedly as he gets back into his seat. "But who the fuck is this and how did she get through the warding on this chamber?"

Holding up my hand, I signal that I need to catch my breath. Connor's arms come around my waist from behind to pull me onto his lap, and I'm finally able to ground myself enough to answer.

"Alpha Elias, meet Cassie," I tell him with a smile. "She is one of the fates and has been working to fix what the woman formerly known as the Goddess broke."

You could hear an amoeba fart on a pinhead with the silence following that statement. Unfortunately, my mother chooses this moment to remind us all that she is still here.

"Dad, why am I here in chains? We are family!" she cries out from the center of the cavern. "I know you hated that I was David's mate, but this is extreme. Can't you let me grieve?!"

"MY SHEILA WAS DAVID'S MATE!"

And we're going to start this again… Eliza glances at me from the other side of the Alpha and we share a look. Using magic, we create a barrier to prevent anyone from the stands making it to the floor until we lift it. As much as she deserves to die, the reason we're here is to get answers first.

Cassie glances at the two of us and nods before sending me a wink and disappearing again. I don't have time to figure out what she was even doing here...

Exasperated, I step out of my mate's embrace to head down onto the floor with my mother. I'm fucking tired of this shit show already. I pull Esther's spirit into the barrier with me to make sure that all of the problems are trapped in here with me. I'm not risking her going after my boy again. It's time to get this fucked up show over with, so Connor can take off my pretty panties with his teeth and we can practice more of our deepthroating skills.

"Mother," I start with her because I frankly don't want to talk to the bitch who abused her sons and still has the audacity to fuck with them after death. "What happened to dad?"

That wasn't the question I wanted to ask. It wasn't even in the front of my head. I should have asked about what the deal was exactly with the fae. I should have asked the real reason I was abandoned by them at fifteen in the middle of fae territory. I should have asked what she spent my entire life running from... But at this exact moment in time, the only thing that is on my mind is that I need to know where my dad is and why *he* stopped loving me.

The child inside of me is dying with each second that I have to wait for an answer. I need to know if I was ever wanted or loved by these people. In the grand scheme of things, it's insignificant, but to me it is the difference between walking away from here a son or a stranger.

I can see her mind working overtime. It's not a trick question. I just want to know what happened to the man who was the only constant in my life for fifteen years...

"Answer the question, Rebecca," Elias growls from somewhere behind me. "Your son can ask whatever he likes in this tribunal, according to the ancient laws. You cannot refuse to answer him."

The woman on the ground looks at me with a sneer. "He's no son of mine," she spits at me. "I may have borne him, but that was an accident."

Her words are like a slap to the face. They shouldn't hurt me anymore, but I can feel it inside. Every time I cried for my mother, praying to an unforgiving universe for my mommy to be like other mommies... The memories flow through unbidden, shredding my heart with every brushoff, every cold gaze, every harsh word...

You might be an accident to her, but you are a miracle for me.

My head snaps back to look at my mate, hearing his voice in my head. I still don't understand why we are able to share our thoughts sometimes, but I truly needed the affirmation of his love. Maybe it's the copy ninja thing... Blinking away the tears in my eyes before they can fall, I offer him a small nod and turn back to the woman on the ground.

"Fine," I say to her. "You are merely the woman who birthed me. Now, what happened to Dad?"

It doesn't escape my notice that she is refusing to answer the question I'm asking when she starts talking about something else completely.

"I never would have come here if it weren't for that dead bitch hitching a ride with me," she mutters. "Like I give a shit about who that sissy fag lets shove a dick up his ass..."

49

SHAUN

The room erupts in growls and I can feel the barrier weakening. Her jabs about my sexuality and my choice of underwear stopped affecting me a long time ago. I've been aware of how my mother felt about my being gay and liking lacy things since she first found my stash. At first, it was just comments against it in general. She didn't direct the criticisms directly to me until her and Dad were leaving me at college.

"Don't go thinking just because you're not under our roof that we'll be alright with you turning yourself into a girl. You are a man, and it's time you act like it," my mother snarls at me while Dad is down at the car getting the last box. "Find a girl. Fuck her. Give me a grandchild... and keep those wolfish perversions away from them."

Dad walks into the room a few moments later, giving me barely enough time to control my shock. I never knew my mother hated my wolf side. Is my love of lace just because of my wolf? If I didn't have a wolf, would I be able to be straight?

My mind is a mess as I wave from the window, watching Dad drive them away from campus. Something tells me this is the last time I'm going to see them. I collapse to the floor in tears and don't even notice when my roommate gathers me up into his embrace.

"Never change who you are, Roomie," Zach whispers as I cling to him. "Your wolf is exactly how he should be, as are you."

I didn't mean to take a trip into my memories. I usually have more control, but this whole situation over the last few days has me all out of sorts. I had honestly forgotten that this woman in front of me made me question who I was for so many years of my life. I had sacrificed my happiness for mere scraps that she wasn't willing to provide.

How did I miss the clues?

"Rebecca Cleary," I lean into her space, forcing her back to fall on her ass. "Answer the fucking question! Where is my father?!"

Her eyes widen in fear, but she stays silent. I need a compulsion that will work on her. Unfortunately, the witches in the room are useless because blood can't compel blood with spells. Magical safeguards and all, but that's also why us witches end up being gaslit by family more often than not...

"Can I help?"

I look to the right and see Reese with another familiar face next to him. I smile at the inclusion of my good friend in these proceedings but wonder how in the hell Celeste got here. She steps through the barrier with very little effort on her part, and for a second, I'm truly happy that she is on our side. I mean, I knew she is powerful, but outside of the equivalent of magical royalty, the barrier my grandmother and I constructed should be impenetrable...

Tucking some hair behind her ear, Celeste gives me a wink before palming the top of my mother's head. I watch the bitch struggle for a few moments, but she eventually calms.

"Ask again, Shaun," Celeste grits out. "I can only bend the geas for a few minutes. I cannot break it."

A geas is the last thing I expected when asking about my dad, but that's not important at the moment. She must really have wanted to keep this secret if she protected it under a geas. I hurry to ask again, knowing this is my only chance to know what happened.

The woman on the ground lets out an inhuman wail before words start tumbling out, almost too fast to make out.

"After the fae gave me the power in exchange for the promise of a witch of my blood, I placed the spell on David. It was only supposed to make him leave with me. We were supposed to have our happily ever after. But then *IT* happened.

"Wolves are supposed to only be able to get their mates pregnant, so as long as I didn't let him bite me, I should have been safe. Instead, I had to birth an abomination to keep him enthralled."

50

CONNOR

It's difficult keeping my wolf in check when I hear Shaun's own mother call him an abomination.

Funny that you have such an issue hearing it all of a sudden, my mother's voice sounds in my head. I can see she is still trapped under whatever magical binding Shaun placed on her, but apparently I don't get to be free of her voice. *You never seemed to have an issue when I used it regarding the one living in my house.*

I wince at the reminder that she regularly called my baby brother an abomination, but I was too self-centered to ever notice. I've seen enough of Ethan's memories over the last couple years to recognize exactly how much I fucked up as his big brother.

You are NOT that thing's brother.

"Fuck you, Esther," I mumble under my breath. Elias and Edward both send questioning looks my way, but I shake my head to let them know I'm fine and that she hasn't escaped.

I turn my attention back to my mate and the carrier that birthed him in time to hear her super villain speech continue, as if she's completely blameless.

"The pregnancy weakened the spell. I originally anchored the spell to the spawn, but David fell in love with it, started to love it more than me. I couldn't have that..."

I can feel Shaun's sorrow through the bond, but I don't want to pause this questioning. Celeste is looking like this is putting a severe strain on her to help, so we need this to move along. I send as much reassurance back to my mate as I can and get rewarded when Shaun's head turns back to me again with a smile. It's a small one, but it brings the light back to his eyes.

"I discovered after a while that I could anchor the spell to pack bonds, so as long as we were part of a pack, David wouldn't question that I was his mate, his *first* priority. Then, *the thing* started to show witch abilities and we got kicked out of every pack we were ever extended an invitation to."

The hatred on her face hurts me to look at. I don't understand how Shaun could be directly in front of it and not fall apart...

"The only bright spot with dragging the thing around was the fact that when the fae came calling, I'd be able to throw him to them. They needed a witch, so what better than give them one who is also a child? I might even have gotten another gift from them for it, but then he fucked things up for me again.

"I made sure Alpha Jameson moved the pack to the closest region to fae territory as possible without being suspicious. It was easy while he was suffering the backlash from Esther Sinclair's influence breaking upon her death. His guilt over cheating on his mate combined with his assumption that his debt to the fae was paid made it very easy to convince him to move where I wanted.

"Then the little shit fucked everything up by getting his wolf after I convinced the Alpha it would be better for us to have a fresh start for the sake of the children. Telling David we were safe right under their noses was easy. Leaving the boy at the school, I left hints to some fae contacts that he was abandoned.

"I was free to be with David," her voice takes on a wistful tone. It's like she's totally lost touch with reality. "Then, about six months ago, that bitch's voice started in on me... telling me I owed her for fucking up her spell. David noticed something was off, but it wasn't until she took over that he changed.

"Last week, I woke up to an empty bed," she says as the water-works start. "The love of my life left me. There was no note. I couldn't track him with my magic. Without him next to me, I didn't have the power. I needed power and needed it from someone no one would care about going missing. So, I called my spawn to fulfill his duty to me for giving birth to him."

The rage inside of me is like nothing I've ever experienced. *Kill her,* my wolf demands of me. I'm right there with him.

No one would miss him? Fuck that! Not counting me, he has been indispensable to Ethan since they first met in elementary school. He singlehandedly saved and delivered the triplets. He saves countless lives as a doctor every single day... He's honestly the single most important person to exist in my whole universe.

51

SHAUN

Only the rage I'm feeling through the bond keeps me from collapsing in on myself while the little boy inside of me crumbles in pain. Yeah, I can see my grandfather and grandmother are upset with what my mother has said, but they don't know me. They just met me yesterday. I don't even know if they even knew of my existence before then.

Just because my son put his dick in you, doesn't mean he knows you. He'll leave you, too.

Even though she got the mechanics wrong as far as whose dick went where, Esther's ghost continues to speak the truths of my deepest fears regarding my mate. Connor doesn't know me, not really. When I was a kid, he ignored me. Over the years, that only continued, sometimes to the point of blatant avoidance. Before these last few days, we barely interacted and the one time we did, I *forced* the bond on him.

Who would ever love an abomination like you? Her voice echoes in my head, and I can't fight anguish.

My mother never wanted me. My best friend didn't even find me to tell me he was alive. No one else stopped to think to inform me either. My father abandoned me to the fae, and then never even looked for me after escaping the brainwashing my mother had him under...

There's a pounding in my head, but I don't care. She's right. They both are. No one cares if I disappear. My grandparents will get over losing the grandson they never knew they had. The world would go on. Ethan has Ric and the babies. Connor will live on for them, I'm sure.

I can do this. I didn't think I could before. I mean how many kids think they can actually kill their parent? But at least this way, I can make sure to take care of both of these bitches. If I tie them to me, when I die, they come with me. They won't hurt another soul...

I hear shouting and the pounding increases, but my mind is made up.

It's better this way. No one gets hurt this way...

52

CONNOR

I've lost the connection to him somehow. The bond is still there, but it's blocked. Elias has shifted and keeps charging at the barrier while the witch Eliza is shaking with the intensity of her concentration to try and break the barrier. The barrier that was keeping him safe moments ago has become the obstacle preventing us from saving him.

I had heard my mother's voice when she whispered to him. I tried to send him assurances, but Celeste's hold on Rebecca broke and a feeling of despair flooded our bond before it shorted out. It's not broken, but I can't feel him like I did. Whatever those two have done to him, it's keeping me out.

A hand on my shoulder pulls my attention away from the sight of my mate on his knees hunched over, in obvious agony. Edward's soft gaze is almost too much for me. I don't need his pity. I need his fucking help!

"I can break into his mind," he tells me. "But depending on what they've done to him, it might be too late. He is contained now, and easy to eliminate as a threat. I don't know what sending you in will do."

Before I can even register my body moving, I am pinning the vampire to the ground by his throat, claws breaking through human hands. My wolf's roar of anger causes cracks to form in the ceiling above us, and Edward raises his hands in surrender. Elias's hand on my shoulder breaks me away from the standoff with the vampire. The room is silent except for the sound of my mate muttering something while he rocks back and forth inside of the barrier.

My eyes meet Edward, and he nods his understanding. I'm going in blind to the maelstrom that is the inside of my mate's head after our mothers fucked with him. Sitting back on my haunches, I have about ten seconds to brace myself and then I feel my consciousness spiraling in an unfortunately not unfamiliar way. This is very similar to what happened when I got kicked out of my body months ago.

It's a very similar process, the vampire's thought grounds me in a way. *I am putting your essence inside of his body, hoping you can stop him from completing the spell he's weaving.*

Spell? What spell?

It will kill him, the vampire sends to me before letting me loose to figure out how to get through to my mate. *It will kill him, but it will save us all in the long run.*

No. It will destroy us all. Even if I don't survive the death of my mate, Ethan will destroy the world to avenge us. The little psycho wouldn't forgive any of us if his bestie dies.

53

CONNOR

I expected going into Shaun and seeing out of his eyes, sharing the space and being one. I did not expect to end up in a forest. Looking around, it all seems too realistic to be real. I think this is what they call the uncanny valley effect. It's creepy as fuck.

I try to see if I can locate where I am, but a whimper behind me has me spinning around in a rush. There... Shaun is curled into a ball trying to hide behind a tree. I make sure he can hear my approach and crouch down next to him. For some reason, he seems smaller to me. I can't figure out why until he lifts his head.

In shock, I fall back on my ass. My mate is only a teenager here. The strong, independent force of a man has been stripped away to reveal this boy with terror and pain in his eyes.

Abomination

Do you want to be a girl? Is that it?

Fucking disgusting!

Cut it off already. That's what you need, right?

Be a fucking man already.

I knew you were fucked up.

At least we don't have to worry about you polluting any bloodlines.

If he wants to take dick, at least let's get some money out of it.

The voices circling around us are spewing such awful statements that I struggle to keep my breakfast from coming back up. Is this what he's heard his whole life?

"Not my whole life," the boy in front of me whispers, putting his head back down on his knees. "Just from the time she realized I like the pretties. She thinks I want to be a woman. Maybe that would have been easier..."

I see the damp spot on the knees of his jeans, and I can't help but pull him into my arms.

"You are perfect, my love," I tell him. "If you were a woman, you wouldn't be my mate. You wouldn't be the one I love. Come back to me.

"P-please don't leave me," I choke out as I let my own tears fall for this broken boy.

Time stretches on in this creepy forest, but I won't release him. This boy needs me, and I'm not ever pulling away from him again. Universe be damned. The bitch can have whatever she wants, but she will *not* take him.

Nothing will take my perfect, beautiful Master from me.

"Glad to hear it," comes a voice from next to where I'm kneeling, and I yelp as I fall over, Shaun still wrapped up in my arms.

The one called Cassie stands up to hop up on a boulder and starts kicking her feet like a child. She may look like a teenager, but from what I understand, she is at the very least older than my grandfather since he is the one who screwed up everything for Ethan.

"Actually," she says picking at some moss on top of her perch, "I'm much older. But that's not important. Right now, we need to fix your mate so that your bitch of a spawner doesn't fuck up my assignments again."

At her words, Shaun pushes himself out of my arms and wipes at his eyes. Squinting at the woman, he takes on a look of suspicion before asking, "Do I know you?"

Fuck! So, not only is he stuck in his teenage self, but he's also stuck with only his teenage memories. I look up at the fate for answers, but she merely shrugs before saying, "I can't actually interfere directly. I did my part by giving you a safe space in his subconsciousness. Anything more intrusive and I can shred your future."

Watching the woman fiddle with the foliage for a moment, I think about what she's just said. It's up to me or we lose our future altogether. No pressure...

54

SHAUN

How many times have I prayed that Connor Sinclair would show up and save me? I started hoping he'd rescue me practically from the moment I first laid eyes on him. My hope in the older boy was proven a pipe dream the first time I noticed Ethan limping to our meeting spot by the pond. Either my knight in shining armor was a bully or he was just as powerless as I am.

Somehow, my knight found me here in my forest. I've been hiding here, trying to escape my mother's voice. It's been chasing me for what seems like days, months, maybe even years. Time has lost its meaning here. I don't know how Connor found his way here, but he needs to go before he hears how worthless I am.

I push at his arms, but they just tighten around me more. I can't take him being kind to me. He's never even said a word to me. Why is he being nice? Does he want me to replace his brother? I can't do that! Ethan is out there somewhere.

"You have to go save Ethan," I whimper. I don't want to be alone again, but my dreams tell me Ethan is more important. He has a destiny to fulfill. I push harder against the chest in front of me, but he won't budge. If I have to use magic, there's a chance I'll hurt him. I don't want to hurt him...

"Let me go, Connor," I plead.

"Never," he breathes into my hair, kissing the top of my head. "I'm yours, now and always. Come back to me, sweetheart."

You think you'll ever get a mate with perversions like this?

You're an abomination!

I should have drowned you as a baby. At least then you wouldn't have had the opportunity to disgrace your father.

The same words from my mother's lips are swirling around, but they are getting softer. There's another voice on the wind, but I can't quite hear it over her.

"I love you. I need you. You're perfect, my Master. You're mine. I'm yours. Use me. Love me."

The words aren't on the wind. They are coming from the man holding me. I tilt my head up to look at the face of the person who is claiming to love me. There's no way it's Connor Sinclair. He's got a mate out there somewhere waiting on him. He's going to go and make gorgeous babies and keep the Beta line of the Jameson pack going.

He notices me looking and chuckles. "Yes, we absolutely will be making some gorgeous babies someday. But first, you need to get your mind back to the present."

I push against him gently, and this time he lets me step back. For the first time since he showed up, I *really* look at him. This isn't the twenty one year old Connor Sinclair. The man in front of me is at least half a decade older. There's no way I've been stuck here for over five years.

Dad would have sent out a search party if I missed his birthday check-in.

Dad...

"What happened to my dad?" I ask, pinching the bridge of my nose. I know that's not the most important thing with missing five years, but judging by the headache that's building, I figure it might be the key to why I'm stuck.

Connor lifts my chin so I am looking at his face. "Your mother had him in thrall for your whole life. Her spell was broken and your father disappeared. That's all we know."

I can see the truth of it in his eyes. As I let those words settle in as truth, more comes back to me. With each flash of memory, my head feels like it's being pierced with an ice pick, but I'm regaining myself piece by piece.

The silver chain whips around my torso, ripping away flesh as I shake it off. Better me than Zach...

"SHAUN!"

My roommate tries to get through the crowd to get to me, but I throw up another barrier to keep him hidden. The fae want him for some reason... more than they want me. But I'm still a child. They will be nicer with me than him.

"Where is he, child?" the figure holding the chain hisses at me. "Tell us and we will not harm you anymore this day."

I snort at the words this being is spouting... "This day? So you can't admit you won't harm me anymore in general?"

The fae looks disgruntled that I caught on. Don't ask me how I can decipher the emotions of a being that looks like a cross between Big Bird's imaginary friend and a trailer park landlord, but apparently I can. I don't know what the reason is that they want Zach, but they are going to need to send someone a bit higher on the food chain to get through me...

"Fuck you, Snuffy," I growl and brace myself for the next blow from the chains.

The memories shift into another and another until I reach this morning

Connor just limps into the bathroom after his "guess" reward. I can't help but chuckle at the thought that he's going to have one hell of a time taking a piss with how hard he is from being spanked. I considered telling him he isn't allowed to find release without me, but I don't want to start orgasm control while under my grandfather's roof. I want to explore that when we have more time and more privacy.

Huh... I'm actually seeing a future with this man now.

"You love him," says a voice from behind me. I don't recognize it, nor do I see anyone in the room. I hear the shower turn on, so it's safe to ask who it is. With the number of people popping in and out and long lost relatives, who knows who it is at this point.

"You never met me, Shaun," the voice says. "But you've made the two most precious boys in my universe smile again. You have my eternal gratitude and any help you need, I'll provide if I can."

Damn ghosts can't even answer a question right...

There's a giggle that reminds me so much of Ethan before she says, "Call me Lizzie," she tells me as the shower turns off. "Remember me. I don't leave my boys alone."

HOLY SHIT! I turn to look at Connor and see him beaming at me. Huh, did he shrink in the last five minutes?

He barks out a laugh and pulls me into his arms for a hug that I gladly return.

"Welcome back, my love."

55

CONNOR

Coming back into my own mind and body, I expected chaos to have erupted while I was helping Shaun inside of his head. Fortunately, it seems like only seconds since I left my body. Sitting back up, I shake my head to reorientate myself to the real world again.

"Damnit!" Edward mutters. "I thought I could get you past the barrier. We can try again. Eliza! I need an assist!"

The vampire starts gesturing for the older witch to come over, but I stand up to wave her off. The shock on Edward's face would be hilarious if the situation were better. Instead, I turned to the barrier and pushed against it.

I don't know who was more surprised that it let me through, Eliza or Rebecca. I had no doubt. Through the memories I saw in the forest, I know now that my purpose is to be here to support my mate however he needs. If that means being a focus and a familiar for his magic, then that's what I am.

"My wolf thanks you for the relief," Shaun mutters as he sits back with a groan. "Why does emotional shit tire me out worse than the physical?"

Knowing the question is rhetorical doesn't stop me from answering. "Because you're strong as fuck, but when it comes to the *emotional shit* you bottle it up until it explodes?"

He chuckles as he takes my offered hand, getting to his feet and planting a kiss on me in front of everyone. Whatever settled inside of him with his memories returning, I'm not going to question it.

"You will NEVER have my son!" My mother's screeching voice causes everyone in the cavern to cringe. Hell, I'm pretty sure people in DC cringed.

I'm ready to defend my mate against my spawner, as Cassie put it, but another voice pipes up that I did not expect.

"Come off it, Esther!" Aunt Lizzie says as she becomes visible and drags my mother back from Shaun and I. "Just because you are jealous that he looks better in the sexy stuff is no reason to pitch a fit."

My jaw falls open and the squeak from the man in front of me makes me pull him tightly to my chest. He might be the Dominant in our relationship, but that doesn't mean he doesn't get comfort when he needs it.

"*Aunt Lizzie!*" I hiss at her to get her attention. She looks back at us, and after a second recognition hits and she appears to be contrite at her outburst. Of course, with her being Ethan's mother, I don't know why I expected an actual apology. Instead, she shrugs and turns back to her sister.

"It's time you left these boys alone, sister of mine," she says to the woman in front of her. "Don't make me get Mom down here, cuz I will."

I ignore the bickering of the two women to look back at my mate's family I left on the other side of the barrier. Eliza and Elias look on in confusion, but Edward... the vampire looks frozen. Oh, shit! The only time he ever saw his daughter was when she was already dead after giving birth to Ethan... and beaten to hell by my grandfather...

"Elizabeth Welling! You don't know a damn thing!" my mother yells, making me return my attention to them. "Richard *was* mine! Anna stole him from me!"

Sure, his fated mate stole him... her and every she-wolf within a fifty mile radius, right?

Shaun's errant thought flickers into my head and I struggle to not let my amusement show on my face. I've heard how delusional my mother was about the old Alpha, but to see it in person... I feel bad for my father. According to what Ethan and Ric told us, they were truly fated mates, but my grandfather made a deal where my mother couldn't recognize it.

"Esther!"

Another woman materializes in front of us, and I can only surmise that I'm looking at my grandmother by the choking noise behind me coming from the vampire king.

"Mommy?" Before our eyes, my mother shrinks in on herself, and I see the woman who was supposed to fall in love with my father. I see the beauty beneath the hate that she couldn't even bring up when she put on her mask for company. "Mommy, why did you leave us?"

The new woman just pats my mother on the cheek before pulling both her girls to her sides. "There is a better place to have this conversation, my lovelies."

Her eyes meet mine with a smile, and I can't help but feel warmth. *Ethan has the same smile...*

"So do you," Shaun whispers to me, wrapping his arm around my waist to help me stay upright. This is too much.

I drop my head to his shoulder, turning to inhale the scent of my mate. I can't help but mutter, "Ethan should be here, too." It's not right that I get to meet our grandmother, but he doesn't. She should know him, and her great-grandbabies, especially her great-granddaughter who is named after her.

"Relax, Connor," she says to me, causing me to slide behind Shaun to keep my chin on his shoulder and still look at her. "Ethan and I have had many conversations. This isn't my first visit this side of the veil, but if you'd been around since the babies were born, you'd know that."

I wince at her admonishment, but with her smile beaming at me I can't stay upset. Now, I understand where my baby brother gets it. Our grandmother has the magic smile that makes you believe that there is nothing bad in the world...

"That she does, Son," Edward says, suddenly beside me. I look and see the barrier is still in place, but somehow the vampire is inside with us. Glancing at my mate, he shoots me a wink. Aw, Shaun is a closet romantic.

56

SHAUN

As cute as the family reunion is, I need answers before the crowd gets restless. I can handle a couple people pounding on the barrier, but if everyone rushes it, I'm not going to be able to hold it. Call me a sucker, but I had to at least let Edward in to see his mate and daughter. The vampire has been like a surrogate grandparent for me this past year. So sue me. I want to give him this.

While Edward takes advantage of the opportunity to hold his mate again, and his daughter for the first time, I turn to Esther. I need to know what part exactly she has played in my mother's actions. I know it's dumb, but I want Esther to be responsible for strangling me. My head knows that the woman who gave birth to me had no qualms killing me, but my heart still wants to believe my mother couldn't do that.

"I know what you want to know," Esther turns to me with a sad smile. I'm sure the joyful reunion of her mother and sister with the vampire brings other memories up for her, but she pushes through to continue. "As much as I don't... *didn't*... want you with my son, I was trying to pull her back from killing you."

At my look of shock, she rushes to continue, "It wasn't because I feel anything for you. It was because my perfect boy would have died with you since you had marked him."

I feel Connor's fingers dig into my hips as my heart cracks back open. I knew it was stupid to hope, but what kid wants to admit their mother wants them dead?

"I would have succeeded if you weren't interfering, you dumbass bitch!" I had forgotten my mother was still chained on the ground.

The growls around the arena all cut short in shock when Olivia, Edward's mate, bitch slaps my mother back to laying on the ground.

"Watch what you call my daughter," she sneers at my mother. "Just because you are too fucking stupid to realize what a blessing a child is, doesn't mean you get to insult other people's children."

In my shock at her response, I don't notice the vampire backing away from the women to stand next to me and Connor. When I move forward to deal with my mother, Edward grabs my arm to hold me back and my mate wraps his arms around me almost to the point of pain. Glancing up at the vampire's face, I am surprised to see fear there.

Turning back to the women, I let my magic pull some of Connor's own flavor of magic through the bond so I can see more of what they're seeing. Relaxing my vision, I start to see shadows that weren't visible to me before. The dead have come to exact a price. Oh, fuck...

"Who called them?" I whisper out of the side of my mouth toward the ancient vampire. "It sure as hell wasn't me..."

Olivia steps into my mother's personal space and lets her see exactly what has come into play. This is the reason their family was almost eradicated. Power over the dead is terrifying. As much as my mother deserves this, I can't let her die yet. The Alpha has to declare the interrogation over. Unfortunately, there's a deep magic that won't let this end without the Alpha's say so. The one who starts the proceedings needs to finish it.

I got my answers. I can't think of anything else I need to know, but I open my mouth to ask.

"Alpha Elias, can the sentence be carried out now or does anyone else have questions for the woman?"

I can't call her my mother at this point. The pain is still too fresh. Turning away from the dead surrounding her, I look to the man who sired my dad. He isn't looking at me or the scene in front of him. His focus is on the shadows behind him. I see him nod before he turns back to the room.

"If there is no one else with questions, I will declare this interrogation complete, and the sentence can be carried out according to the wishes of the wronged."

I hold my breath, expecting Sheila's father to have another outburst, but he seems content with the fact that the woman on the ground has soiled herself. Turning to face Reese and Celeste, she smiles at me while he bows his head in deference to me. I let my gaze run around the room, but no one else steps forward to ask anything. Looking back to the Alpha he raises his hand palm up, as if he's handing the responsibility to me.

"I have a question," my mate utters before I declare her sentence.

He doesn't look at me, but glares at her while he asks, "If he had not had magic as a toddler, would you have let Shaun live?"

The look on her face is answer enough.

"Olivia? Please?" I ask. "I can't do it myself. Gods be damned, she's still my mother to me..."

The ghost of my mate's grandmother gives me a sad smile before nodding that she will take the life of the woman who gave birth to me. I feel her fingers slide down my cheek in a comforting gesture as I close my eyes to lean back against Connor's chest. Fuck, I don't want to do this...

Seconds or hours later, it doesn't matter. I'll never forget the sounds of my mother's screams as the dead ripped her apart.

57

CONNOR

I don't need to ask when the barrier comes down. I lift Shaun into my arms and carry him from the cavern back to our room. I could feel his pain at the sounds of his mother's death. I was happy to see him closing his eyes. I watched so he didn't have to, and the sight will stay with me...

That is the power that lives in my veins. That is what my mother could have been capable of...

That thought has me stopping in my tracks. I clutch my mate closer and lean my face down to give him a peck on his forehead. The woman could have destroyed us all. We are damn lucky she didn't have the knowledge that Olivia has.

"Your family's ability can't be used in malice," Shaun mumbles into my chest as I cross the threshold into the room. I kick the door shut behind me so that I don't have to let go of my mate for us to have privacy. "To use the dead as a weapon would result in them turning on the wielder. Your mother's soul would have been shredded if she tried."

At the bed, I lay myself down and reposition Shaun into a more comfortable position, stretched out beside me with his upper body resting on my chest. Running my hands up and down his back, I feel him start to relax into my embrace.

"Since when do you know so much about my family's abilities?" I ask him when it becomes obvious he isn't going to volunteer anything else.

He lifts his head up to glance at my face before snuggling back into my shirt. I almost wish I had thought of taking it off before climbing on the bed, but that would have required letting go of him. I'm not ready to do that yet, not so close after almost losing him.

Shaun mumbles something into my chest that suspiciously sounds like a curse, but when he lifts his head up again, he's smiling sheepishly.

"Since the incident with the gods," he breathes out after a pause.

"You mean the incident where my mother possessed me, I nearly killed you, and you claimed me against my wishes to save my life?"

He pushes up to loom over me with a look of reprimand on his face. "Wanna try that again, boy?"

I can't help but let my smile come forward as I shake my head. I love it when he gets all growly with me. His show of dominance is all the proof I need that we will be alright, even with the horrors of this day.

He lowers himself back to rest on my chest, mumbling something about brats and spankings. I'm ready whenever he is, but for now we need cuddles and rest.

"I wanted to make sure that you both were safe," he says into the dimness of the room long after I thought he had drifted off. "Magic like that, necromancy, was banned for a reason. Your family line is the only one that has the ability without sacrificing a life for the capability. At the time, I didn't know you guys were Hurleys…"

The only thing I could do is continue to run my hands up and down his back, giving comfort to my mate. As far as I'm concerned, I'm not a witch. I'm a wolf. These abilities don't matter to me. I'll never use them.

"I was afraid that your mother killed your father for the magic," he whispers and my hands still on his back. "I didn't want you to know about it if it was true. I didn't want to completely ruin your memories of your parents."

My hands resume their course as I lift my chin toward the ceiling.

This man spent months doing research into this ability, not because of the threat it posed to us all, but because he worried about *my feelings* regarding my irredeemable mother. Nothing could ever excuse her actions toward Ethan, but a small part of me is thankful that she wasn't a murderess.

Small blessings...

58

SHAUN

I can feel the relief flowing through the bond. As much as we've all learned about Esther Sinclair over the last year, and how little there has been to redeem her, I know Connor still loves his mother deep down. I mean, I can't fault him for loving her when I am here grieving the monster that gave birth to me. At least his mother loved him in her own twisted way.

Connor's hands still on my back again, and this time I look up to make sure he's actually asleep before I do anything else embarrassing, like confess my undying love and need to put a collar or tattoo on him to mark him as mine to more than just the supernatural community. Sliding out from under his arm, I can't help but stare at the sleeping man who has changed my life, saved my life, so many times over.

"Who's that?" I ask my new friend Ethan as he releases me from our hug in front of the diner.

Ethan looks behind him to see the last of the wolves racing into the forest. His smile is brilliant when he faces me again. "You mean the red one that has the black tips?"

At my nod, my friend starts bouncing on his tip-toes in excitement.

"That, my friend, is the bestest big brother in the world!" He grabs my

wrist and pulls me off toward the woods in another direction. "Connie is the greatest! Let's go to my secret spot and I'll tell you all about how he got me my very own nightmare hunter."

The copper wolf thinks he's clever, hiding behind the bushes, but it's obvious Connor suspects something. I know Ethan didn't tell the truth to his family about how his bike was broken. That was obvious by how no one got in trouble and my friend looks like he hasn't slept in days.

"You need to tell someone what really happened, E-man," I try to convince him as I throw another pebble into the pond, sending the fish scattering. "You know I got your back."

Ethan looks like he's going to be sick for a moment before he answers me.

"It's okay, Shaun. I'm handling it," he whispers as he leans his head against my shoulder. I'm younger than he is, but he's so much smaller than I am. "I don't want trouble to find you, too."

The growl from behind the bush makes me wish I had a wolf, too. Maybe then, I could protect my best friend from the bullies intent on hurting him.

"He's not dead!"

I scream in the face of the Alpha, not caring at all that I'm supposed to show him respect. If the man wants respect, he needs to prove he deserves it.

"You left him behind! HE'S NOT DEAD!"

I can hear the commotion in the hall behind me, but my focus is on the coward in front of me as he raises his hand to strike me... He is actually going to hit me...

I can feel my magic rising to protect me. A blow from a full-grown man would be enough to seriously me, seeing as I'm barely twelve, but a werewolf? And an Alpha on top of it? I'm dead. My magic will help me survive, but at what cost... I throw my arms over my head and pray that I don't blow anyone or anything up.

I hear the blow connect, but don't feel anything. Peeking out between my forearms, I see Connor Sinclair on the ground in front of me, blood trickling from his mouth. I back away in horror and shame from the sight in front of me.

I hear the Alpha Mate yelling for me to come back, but it's barely audible over the roaring of my magic in my head. Connor saved my life. Why wasn't he there to save Ethan?

"Why do I even bother hiding from the fae?" I ask Zach for the fourth time tonight. I'm tired of hiding. I've spent my entire life hiding.

Hiding from whoever is hunting my family.

Hiding the fact that I want to wear soft, pretty, and sexy underwear.

Hiding that I crave to control someone physically stronger than myself.

Hiding that the only man I ever want to give me that control is Connor Sinclair... the only man I can't have.

"Dude," Zach reprimands me as he snatches the bottle of vodka out of my hand. "Where in the hell did you get a bottle of hundred proof vodka?! You're sixteen!"

I shrug and wave my hand toward our small cubby shelves we got on clearance last year. Two more bottles appear on top. I almost fall off my bed in my attempt to grab one, but settle back into my pillows to continue my bender.

It's been five years since my best friend disappeared, and still no one cares... I even held out hope that maybe if I didn't send this year's letter and email, Connor would be concerned about me and finally go searching. But of course he didn't.

Instead, the man in question was here in the city with one of the whiny bitches from the pack. Of course he moved on. My dream man is just that... a dream.

Taking a swig, I sputter and cough at the unexpected taste. I glance down at the label and realize that I got gin instead of vodka this time.

"Unless you're trying to kill yourself and your wolf by getting alcohol *poisoning, I suggest you cool it," Zach says as he pulls this bottle away from me as well. "Your wolf isn't fully matured yet, remember?"*

I lay back against my pillows and throw my arm across my eyes to hide the tears, but soon anger takes their place. Jumping out of bed, much to the surprise of my suddenly overly responsible roommate, I stomp over to my desk to boot up my laptop.

Connor WILL be hearing from me this year... and every six months from now until Ethan is home where he belongs. The asshole might have moved on, but I won't ever let him forget. He will be my mission until we can get my bestie back where he belongs.

What the fuck was that? I haven't gotten lost in my own memories like that in... well, never.

Sorry, Bestie. I'm still learning how strong I am now that I'm not stuck in the deal. I never knew you went through that.

Hearing Ethan's voice in my head is enough to make me smile. I can tell he's on the verge of his little persona, which means he's stressing out about something.

What's up, E-man? Why not call on the phone? I send back to him. In person, we'll have these mental conversations when we don't want others to listen in, but I don't see a reason why we need to use the mental stuff when we're in separate states, unless... *Are you hiding things from your Daddy again?*

I can hear his giggle before his voice comes through again, *Nope, but you didn't answer your phone and Connie's goes straight to voicemail and I got worried.*

Huh... Speaking of my phone... I start digging through my backpack, but don't find it. Looking at the nightstand, I see Connor's phone, but that's it. I'm beginning to think that Cassie forgot to inform Ethan that we were alright after her impromptu visit last night.

I think I lost my phone when my mother kidnapped me, I tell him as I start to repack my bag. I'm not planning on sticking around here much longer. I miss home. *Connor's asleep right now, but I guess the battery died on his.*

YOU WERE KIDNAPPED?!

The intensity of his thought through the mindspeak is enough to make me jump and drop my bag, which in turn wakes up the gorgeous man in the bed. Connor looks around in a panic but relaxes when he sees me. He raises his eyebrow at the bag in my hand as I pick it back up, but I wave his concern away and place the bag next to the door.

Long story, Ethan. But the short version is that my mother is no longer a problem, and we're coming home.

Connor wraps his arms around me as I climb back onto the bed while I listen to my best friend celebrating in my head. Turning to place a kiss on my mate's forehead, I whisper to him, "Let's go home, baby."

59

SHAUN

Leaving is easier said than done. First, there was the huge dinner that everyone insisted needed to happen to close out the interrogation and everything that went on. Then, there was the celebration to reflect that the Alpha's line hadn't died out after all. *Then*, there was the contingent that wanted to make a big deal over the fact that I'm only a beta and unable to inherit the title of Alpha...

That one got Connor's hackles raised on my behalf, which ,although sexy as all hell, was unnecessary. I have absolutely zero desire to run a pack. The only wolf I am in charge of is my mate. That is enough for me.

"His mate is an alpha. Problem solved."

Both of our wolves react to those words and our growls drown out all speech in the banquet hall we have been in since the dinner started over three hours ago.

"I am the Beta of the Jameson Pack," Connor snarls into the silence. "I have no claim to be Alpha Heir, nor do I want to usurp my mate's birthright. To even suggest that is tantamount to treason for both packs."

I pull him into my side and chuckle at the way he is still bristling on my behalf. "Easy, boy. You're the only wolf I ever intend to boss around, and the only place I want to be is back home."

Elias signals for the two of us to follow him out of the hall, so I pull my still grumbling mate along to the Alpha's office. After taking a seat on the loveseat in the corner, Connor pulls me into his lap. He's still surly after the last hour or so of forced socialization in the other room, so I just pat his hand and relax into his embrace. How in the hell has this man managed to be Beta for the last nine years if he hates this stuff so much?

My grandfather pours us all a drink from his private stock and adds a fourth glass to the coffee table before taking a seat in one of the chairs across from us. I don't even have the opportunity to get the question out before a hidden door opens behind the bookcase...

Why is it always the bookcase? I hear Connor's words in my head, which makes me chuckle.

The laughter dies in my throat when the man steps from the shadows. My father is here. The man who abandoned me to fend for myself at fifteen. The man who ran from my mother *months ago* but never bothered to come to me.

I don't know what to say. I don't even think before the words are tumbling out.

"Was it even you who texted and sent the cards?"

What am I saying? This isn't what I want to know! I want to ask him why he didn't fight harder. I want to know how he could leave me behind. I want to ask him if he ever really loved me or if it was all just a byproduct of some stupid spell. I need to know if he wanted me, or if I was just something thrust upon him.

Connor holds me tighter and lays a kiss on the back of my neck to calm me. I know my turmoil is surging through the bond, but he is trying to give me back a calm I don't know if I want to feel. I want to be numb to this man, but at the same time I want him to suffer.

"You are my son, Shaun," the man says as he takes the other seat on the other side of the table. Side by side, I can see the resemblance between Elias and David, but it doesn't matter. "We are family whether you like it or not."

My body goes rigid at his words. *Whether I like it or not?* Is that truly how this man sees it?

"My family is made up of the people who love me unconditionally," I snarl as I pull my mates arms away so that I can stand. "My family are the ones who have held me when I cried over the parents who never took my side when things happened outside of my control.

"My family are the ones who helped piece me back together after my parents abandoned me in the middle of fae territory to fend for myself. My family are the ones who protected me, even when it was safer for everyone to leave me to die...even if it meant they would die, too.

"*MY FAMILY*," I take a breath to calm down because I don't need to be losing control of my magic over this. "My family are the ones who showed me it's not wrong to want to wear the clothes I want or love the way I want. My family love me for who I am, not what blood runs in my veins."

The man in front of me is a stranger. The Dad I remember would be ashamed of his behavior. The man sitting across the table is only showing confusion.

I sigh and sit down on the loveseat next to Connor. Looking into my mate's eyes, I don't even turn to address the other men in the room before I say, "My *family* is back in the Jameson Pack and we're going home to them now."

60

CONNOR

Shaun grabs my hand and goes to stand back up, but I pull him back down. His attention was focused on his father. My attention was on the Alpha in the room. While David might not give a shit about his son, Elias is showing that he loves his grandson already. The glare I get from my mate doesn't stop me from keeping him in the room. I know this is the right thing to do.

"David, why is Shaun's middle name Eliazor?" I ask before my mate tries to get up again.

There's pain in the man's eyes, but the rest of him is the perfect appearance of nonchalance as he responds, "His mother chose his first name. I chose his middle name as a way to honor both sides of his heritage. She didn't even know about his middle name until the birth certificate came in the mail."

A ghost of a smile plays on his lips, but the derisive snort from my side makes it disappear.

"Most of the last twenty two years is hazy, but the memories that come through clearest are the ones where my pride as a father over-powered everything else," he says matter-of-factly. "I spent the last few months just trying to figure out how long I had been bespelled and where the fuck I even was. It took a solid six weeks to figure out if David Cleary was even my real name."

Looking at my mate, I would think he's still angry at the man in front of us. Through the bond, I feel his confusion. Personally, I hate the man in front of us just a bit right now. Instead of coming forward right away, he waited. Instead of being truthful, he's hiding himself. Knowing this is how he was going to be, why the fuck did he bother coming forward at all?

Mate doesn't need him. Mate only needs pack, my wolf grumbles in my head.

We're not wasting any more time here. It's time to get us back home where we belong, so I stand and pull Shaun up to his feet next to me. Turning to Alpha Elias, I give the courtesy his position deserves, both as the Alpha of this pack and as the grandfather of my mate.

"Alpha Elias, thank you for your hospitality and assistance. I hope we can see more of each other in the future. I'm sure my Alpha and his mate will welcome you into our territory with open arms when-ever you wish to visit your grandson."

Turning to my mate's father, I add, "David, get your head out of your ass."

With that parting shot, I pull my mate from the room and gather his bag. It's not until we're outside that I remember that neither one of us has a vehicle here...

"Forget something, Beta?"

I turn just in time to catch the keys flying at my head. Shaun lets out a chuckle at the sight of our friend, and Ethan's cousin, Josh lounging on the hood of my truck.

"My uncle asked me to bring it to you guys after Ethan told us you were planning to head on back tonight," the vampire says, sliding down from his perch and turning to the man next to me. "And *your baby* is currently on the back of a tow truck headed for your lover's driveway, but I can have the destination changed to a guy I know if you'd prefer a professional work on it?"

Shaun rushes forward to put the vampire in a headlock. "Ain't no grubby vamp gonna get their claws into Baby," he laughs out as the two of them start to play wrestle.

Throwing the backpack into the backseat, I call out to Josh to see if he needs a ride back home, but he says it's faster for him to run it. I get the feeling something else is going on there, but I just want to get on the road.

After saying goodbye to our friend, we climb into the truck. Taking Shaun's hand in mine, I kiss his knuckles before pulling away from the house.

"So..." I glance at him as he's fiddling with my radio. "Your place or mine?"

61

SHAUN

The drive back to South Carolina is a lot easier when you aren't by yourself, freezing your nuts off. It's difficult to believe it's only been a few days since my mother's call sent me running away from the only real family I've ever known. I'm never making that mistake again. Nothing will pull me away from my mate and the foundation we've all built up in the Jameson Pack.

Looking over at the man napping in the passenger seat, I'm reminded yet again that Cassie really seems to want us to succeed and work out. Never in a million years did I think that not only would I be mated to Connor Sinclair, but that he is my perfect match in every conceivable way.

"Well, duh!"

The voice from the backseat startles me, but I manage not to swerve the truck too badly. At least we're driving at night and there aren't that many cars on the interstate right now.

"Damnit, Cassie!" I hiss at the girl giggling silently in the backseat. "I don't need to fucking wreck his truck the first time I get to drive it!"

I've never gotten to drive a vehicle that isn't falling apart around me, and I'd rather not blow my future opportunities by demolishing this one. It takes a second to realize I have no clue why the fate has decided to make an appearance this time.

"Why are you here, Cass?" I ask, glancing over to make sure Connor is still asleep. I think she does something to make sure we have our privacy, but I'm almost afraid to ask.

She picks at her cuticles for a while before giving me a hard glare and says, "You haven't made your babies, yet. I'm on a schedule, you know..."

"How the fuck are we supposed to make babies?" I ask her, taking the exit ramp from the interstate. We are less than an hour away from the point that I have to wake up Connor to decide where we are going to sleep the rest of the night away. "In case you forgot, neither of us is an omega. Seems like you or your siblings fucked that one up if our babies are so important."

Cassie cackles behind me... legit evil movie witch vibe cackles.

"Silly Werewitch," she singsongs. "You just need a vessel. Who do you know with a womb that would carry a couple kids for you?"

My first thought is Ethan, but after his last pregnancy, I refuse to put my best friend through that kind of terror just for my sake. I know for a fact he would agree, not just for me, but because the babies would be Connor's as well. But no... I'll never ask that of Ethan.

Just then, my phone rings, waking Connor up next to me. Glancing in the rearview mirror, I notice Cassie wink at me and then disappear. I fucking hate that she does that...

"You gonna answer that?" my mate grumbles as he adorably rubs the sleep from his eyes.

I hit the answer button on the console screen even though I'm legitimately curious as to how my phone got in the truck for the Bluetooth to pick it up. When the call connects, background sounds of the hospital filter through the truck's speakers.

"Dude! Where have you been?" Mick's voice pours out above the chaos before it abruptly quiets down. "I'm hiding from the grouch. Savvy is going postal without you around, man."

And now the visit from Cassie makes sense...

"Can you put her on the phone, Mouse?" I ask while Connor

reaches over to reclaim my hand now that he is awake. "I need to talk to her about something."

I hear the chaos pick back up in the background along with some cursing and apologies from the man on the other end of the line before I hear the harsh tone from the she-wolf in question.

"*What*" she snarls into the phone and I feel the need to physically jerk back from the sound of her voice.

"Somebody's grumpy," Connor mumbles as he pulls out his own phone to fiddle with.

Savannah legitimately growls on the other end before responding. "You want grumpy? I surpassed grumpy days ago, Beta brat, so keep it up and I'll beat your ass like I've been dying to since the last time we faced off."

Oh, shit... Time to put the mediator hat on.

"Sav, honey," I gentle my tone as much as I can without going totally soft. "When was your last cycle?" It never goes over well when a man asks a woman about her cycle, but this is definitely important, both for the huge favor I want to ask her as well as her own health. As healthcare professionals, we tend to forget about our own health in favor of treating our patients, so we tend to help each other out with keeping track.

The gasp on the other end of the conversation tells me all I need to know. Her wolf is going into her fertile period, but the woman hasn't made any concessions for that. Yeah, that would make her a grouch and a beast at work...

"Oh, my gods, Shaun," she practically sobs. "I am so sorry. I owe so many people apologies."

Laughing a bit at my friend's foolishness, I take the turnoff to head toward the pack, instead of my cabin. Connor's joy that I'm heading to his house flows into me though the bond.

"I'm gonna cut this call short, hun, but I have a huge favor to ask... like Godzilla huge," I tell her as I smile at my mate. "Have you ever considered surrogacy?"

EPILOGUE
CONNOR

Helping Savannah down from my truck, I can't believe how my life has turned out. A year ago today, I thought I had lost everything. My mate couldn't stand to even look at me. My baby brother was dead. I had nothing to live for, except the three amazing angels who came into the world that day.

Now, not only is my brother *not* dead, but we have probably the best relationship we've ever had. There are still things I know he keeps hidden from me to try and protect me, but I've been working on breaking him of that habit. Ric is working on it as well. I might have fallen hard into depression, but as long as I don't wall myself off again, it should all stay on track...

As the she-wolf carrying our twins waddles her way into the house from the garage, I notice my bike is missing from where I usually keep it parked. I'm extremely picky about who touches my motorcycle since it was the first gift I received from my baby brother that he picked out himself.

Hanging my keys on the hook in the kitchen, I call out for Shaun to see if he's home and ask about the bike. We're supposed to be heading over to Ric and Ethan's place for the party in a few hours. When I get no answer, I shrug and assume he is the one who took the bike out. He is on the *very* short list of people I let ride it.

Savannah waddles into the kitchen as I hear the sound of running water from the direction of the hallway. She must have needed the half-bath...

"Your boys had better figure out a better place to play soccer than my bladder," she grumbles before burying her head in the freezer with a sigh. "I don't know what I want more. The cold or the ice cream."

I chuckle when she emerges with three pints, all different flavors, and heads back down the hallway toward the living room. Shaking my head, I pick up the mail on the counter and begin to sort through it. This is my routine. Routines help keep the depression and guilt at bay. I still have dark moments, but my mate and family are there to bring me back when I can't handle it on my own.

Speaking of my mate, I pull my phone out of my pocket to give him a call, but before I can even pull up his contact information, I get a text from Ric.

> What the fuck did you do now?
>
> Why is your bike in my pool on the day of my kids' birthday party?

My wolf rises to the surface, and I barely manage to maintain human form as the panic builds...

The sound of the garage door opening has me tearing the connecting door off its hinges. Fuck it. I'll fix it later...

Shaun's car pulls into the farthest bay in the garage. I hadn't even noticed it was empty since I was so focused on the bike being gone. Normally, I would notice the Impala missing on the other side of the Tesla, but between the pregnant lady needing the facilities and the motorcycle, I didn't even look.

My mate barely has the key out of the ignition when I reach in to yank him out of the car and into my arms. I don't know if it was fear that he was angry at me or if it was fear that something happened to him. But the only thing I felt was overwhelming terror when I read that text from my best friend.

"What's this?" Shaun asks while awkwardly petting me on the back.

I let him go and he wipes my cheeks gently. I hadn't even noticed I was crying. He pulls me back into an embrace. Only this time, he's comforting me while I get a handle on myself.

He's safe. He's here. He didn't leave me...

"Connor?" he asks, rubbing my back soothingly. "Where's the Ducati?"

ABOUT THE AUTHOR

I am a dog mom living it up in the insanity that is Northeast Ohio. When I'm not documenting the exploits of the characters in my head, I'm either binge reading the works of other amazing authors or losing my voice at hockey games. I'm horribly addicted to coffee, anime, and Asian dramas in addition to building my ever-growing stuffie army.

To break it down to the basics, I am a neurospicy aceflux demirom hetero cis woman middle who writes about people (mostly LGBTQIA+) finding love and purpose through unexpected means. Almost all of my stories involve some facet of BDSM, but the heart of the matter is the characters and their growth.

K.A. Bauer is the paranormal alter ego of Kate Bauer. I guess you could say Kate lives in this reality while K.A. is in a reality where mythical creatures and magic exist and fate makes finding true love easier.

For the latest news on releases and appearances, check out my website www.authorkabauer.com

For links to all of my socials and to sign up for my newsletter, check out my linktree at https://linktr.ee/authorkabauer

I can be found on most social media sites under the username
@authorkabauer

K.A. BAUER BOOKS

Alpha's Little Psycho Series
Alive
Holly Jolly Psycho (Novella)
Unburied
Afraid
Complete Series Omnibus

Jameson Pack Series
Fated Mistake
Doctor Mate
Half Mate
Learned Fate

*All of my books that are not under an exclusivity clause are also
available direct from my store*
www.authorkabauer.shop

KATE BAUER BOOKS

Manor Drive Series
A Little Discovery
Drag Me Up
Pet Project
Teddy Tea Time
Night Shift
No Pain, No Gain

Wrenshaw University Series
Freshman Fifteen
Injured Reserve
Professor's Pet
Too Many Men

MR DRAG Series
Wish Upon DeStarr

All of my books that are not under an exclusivity clause are also available direct from my store
www.authorkabauer.shop

www.ingramcontent.com/pod-product-compliance
Lightning Source LLC
Chambersburg PA
CBHW051506260626
47162CB00008B/2840